THE

BACKUP

PLAN

By

Harold Burt-Gerrans

COPYRIGHT

This book is a work of fiction. References to real people, events, establishments, organizations or locations are intended only to provide a sense of authenticity and are used fictitiously. All characters, incidents and dialogue are drawn from the author's imagination and are not to be interpreted as real.

Published by: H. Burt-Gerrans, 2017

Cover Artwork provided by: Martin Schrimpel

Paperback ISBN: 978-0-9959321-1-1

Blurb.ca ISBN: 978-0-9959321-3-5

The Backup Plan

Contents

Forward

This novel is a fictional account of an absolutely true Canadian achievement in World War II.

It is based on events which occurred at the University of Toronto in the early 1940s.

Dr. Norman E. Burt-Gerrans

Dedication

Dedicated to the memory of my friend Tim and my son's friend Nick. Their short lives inspired characters in this novel.

And mostly, dedicated to the memory of my father, Dr. Norman Edward Burt-Gerrans. Our last private conversation was about this book.

Dad, don't do anything I wouldn't do.....

This page intentionally left almost blank.

The Backup Plan

Chapter 1

Doc Beege was old. Not ancient, just retirement old. Tall and slender, he looked well for his age. If it wasn't for the completely full head of gray hair and moustache, he could pass for a much younger man. Technically, he was Dr. George Beege, Chemistry PhD, retired, but everyone still called him 'Doc'. Perhaps the funniest thing about it was that his son, Neville, was also Dr. Beege, except he was Dr. Beege MD and nobody called him 'Doc'. Neville didn't know how his dad got that nickname, and when asked, his dad always just said, "It's from the war." Doc Beege was sitting in his favourite chair at his son's home, a spring rocking chair in the family room where he could watch the TV.

Doc Beege looked around the room and thought that his son had done well for himself. The house was a typical two story home with a kitchen, family room, den, two bedrooms and a bathroom on the main floor, two more bedrooms and a bathroom on the upper floor. The upper floor was not as big as the main floor. Neville and his wife, Mary, used the master bedroom on the main floor and Henry, their son, had the bedroom beside them. The upstairs was almost like a guest apartment. Nobody typically went there except Doc Beege or Mary's parents when they were visiting.

Doc Beege had a favourite chair at his own house too, but this chair was the one he enjoyed when visiting Neville's family. He had been visiting for several weeks now. Sitting on his lap was his grandson Henry. Henry was listening intently as Doc Beege discussed the polymerization process of nylon. Henry was four and a half years old.

"Dad? What are you doing?" asked Neville as he came into the room. Neville was the spitting image of his dad. He was also tall and slender and even had a similar moustache and hair style, although his was still dark brown.

"Just explaining nylon polymers to Henry."

"Dad, he's not even in Kindergarten. He can barely pronounce 'Polymers'."

"Tsk Tsk," Doc Beege replied. "You underestimate your own son. He's smart, I can see it in him already, maybe as smart as Einstein."

"Yes Dad, he is smart. He walked early, he talked early, he learned to count early. He uses reasoning already. I saw him outsmart you the other day when you made the milkshakes. You put some in a short fat glass and some in the tall skinny glass, just enough that it was a little higher than the level of the short fat glass. You thought he would pick the tall glass because the level was higher, but he knew there was actually more in the other glass." Neville shook his head as he stifled a laugh. "PhD outsmarted by a K.I.D."

"But," Neville continued, "it might be a little early to draw comparisons with Einstein."

"Perhaps, but I think Albert would agree with me, especially if he knew about the milkshakes."

"Albert? You're on a first name basis with Einstein?" Neville scoffed at his Dad's comment.

Doc Beege began bouncing Henry on his knees. Henry was giggling.

"Of course I am," Doc Beege replied, smiling at Henry. "I knew Dr. Einstein. We're both professors. You met him too, once, when he visited the university. Ah, but you were so young, maybe about two or three. It was so long ago now, it's hard to remember exactly when. I'm sure you won't remember."

"No, I don't remember that. But I will concede that Henry loves to listen to you rattle on about things, even if he doesn't understand what a polymer is."

"Polymers make nylons like mom's clothes!" exclaimed Henry, prompting laughter from both doctors.

Later, after dinner and after Henry had gone to bed, Neville asked, "Are you sure you want to go home this evening? You know you could never wear out your welcome here."

"Yes, I'm sure. It's been almost a month now. I should stay at home for a while. I need to do some of the work around the house that's been piling up. And visit some of my friends. Gears and Bounce will be wondering where I am. At our age, we have to visit each other often, each visit might be the last. You never can know. I'll stay there a while, then come back here for a while again."

"Henry will miss you."

"He knows I'll be back," Doc Beege scoffed.

Shortly afterwards, Neville loaded the suitcases into the trunk of the Mercedes Benz; a black Mercedes with a red interior, a fine example of German engineering. Being a doctor in a small city did not afford many luxuries, so the Mercedes was one that Neville sacrificed other luxuries to have.

The two men piled into the car and within a few minutes Neville guided the smooth mechanical marvel onto the highway heading towards Toronto. Although it was summer and the sun still had not set, the evening was darkened by black clouds, and it was evident that a storm was imminent.

"So," Neville opened the conversation, "how well did you know Einstein?"

"I guess the best description would be 'Colleague'. I mean, we knew each other professionally. We were brought together through common research before the war."

"World War II?" Neville asked.

"Yes. During the war, the University of Toronto and most universities were conducting research for the atomic bomb and other war related things. He really wasn't directly involved with the development of the atom bomb, but in the late 1930s and early 1940s his research did have him communicating with Chemistry and Physics professors throughout Canada, USA and England. He visited University of Toronto on several occasions, once being a time you happened to be with me on campus. That's when you met him. But, we became friends on a very casual level. We occasionally exchanged letters after the war. Of course, that ended in the mid 1950s."

The car sped down the highway as they spoke. Ahead, under the black sky, the rain was falling. It appeared like a watery curtain across the road. Neville switched on the headlights and the wipers just as the car drove through the wall of water. The radio had been providing some light background behind the conversation, but now, with the tapa-tapa-tap of the rain on the metal of the car body compounding the background noise, Doc Beege clicked the radio off.

"So, your research work during the war was used to develop the A-Bomb?"

"Hah," snorted Doc Beege. "Some maybe. There was research work provided from many universities. I don't recall a specific discovery made by the team at U of T, but maybe something small could have been of value to the Manhatten Project."

The storm was growing stronger after passing through the wall of water. The rain was coming down hard and visibility was down to just a few feet in front of the car. Neville had slowed considerably. It was clear that the normally hour and a half drive to mid-Toronto was going to take over two and a half hours if the rain kept at this strength.

"Was all your work towards the A-bomb during the war?"

Doc Beege didn't answer. He just stared out of the side window, watching the fields pass by for several minutes, or at least what appeared to be fields in the downpour. He couldn't see past the shoulder of the road, but he knew the area was mostly farmland along the highway. The rain was almost torrential now, coming down so hard that the tapa-tapa-tap sound seemed to echo through the car.

"I don't think you should be driving in this. It's dangerous. Do you have to drive back home tonight? Or can you stay at my place overnight?" Doc Beege asked Neville.

"I can stay. I'll just get up early to drive back."

"Good. Then we can take all the time we need. Why don't you pull over onto the shoulder under the next bridge and wait for the rain to ease. It will give us some time to talk while we wait," Doc Beege said, pointing down the road ahead of them.

"Sure," Neville replied. Shortly, the next overpass appeared and he turned on the four-way flashers and pulled the car gently onto the shoulder and rolled to a stop under the bridge. The rain was still torrential, but at least now it was not hitting the car and the noise level was much better.

"Do you remember much about the war?"

"Not really. I was too young, in kindergarten, and we were here, on this side of the ocean. I think I can remember that we had air raid drills at school and there was a big siren on the roof. We all would get on the floor, under our desks. Silly that we thought those flimsy wooden desks could shelter us during a bombing. But of course, there never was an actual air attack."

"You know that D-Day, June 6th, 1944, was a major turning point of the war?"

"Sure. They covered that in History class. England, USA, and Canada planned a massive offensive. Months went into the planning and some things were done to confuse the Germans into thinking that the offensive would not be on the Normandy beaches. They threw almost all of their combined strength into the landing. It was successful and that gave the foothold to advance through Europe and eventually win the war."

"Yes, that's basically what happened. Did they teach about what would have happened if the Germans had successfully defeated the attack?"

"Not really," Neville said with a light laugh. "But the implication was that if the landing had failed, England would fall shortly afterwards and maybe I would have been learning to speak German in school."

"Yes, most historians would probably agree with you," Doc Beege replied, joining in the light laughter. They chuckled for a few moments. Then Doc Beege looked up with a more serious look on his face.

"But I can tell you for an absolute fact, it would never have happened. There was a secret backup plan."

Chapter 2

Neville looked at his father, thinking he must be joking.

"A secret backup plan? Was it such a secret that no one ever mentioned it in our history courses?"

"It's not in your history books. Lots of things from the wars are not in your history books. Firstly, the history books are written by those who won the wars, or at least survived, so only half to two-thirds of the truth is captured. Every government has records and secrets that are classified as top secret and are sealed. Some records are sealed for fifty years, others for a hundred, some permanently. This one falls into that last category," Doc Beege said indignantly.

"I've held this secret for over thirty years. I may be the only one still alive that knows all the details. I don't think the secret should die with me. If you're interested, I'll tell you provided that you keep the secret until after I'm gone. After that, you can do with it as you please."

"Well, with that kind of introduction, who could not be interested? Of course I'm interested. And if the secret is truly that important, then you should probably pass it on. But if the records are sealed, aren't you violating some kind of national security?"

"That's why you can't mention it to anyone until after I die. I've been sworn to secrecy on this. I don't know the rules, maybe it would be considered treason to release the secret. But I'm not fond of the idea that these events are buried in some files that may never be read again. Maybe at some time in the future, this information may be of value, but it will only be of value if someone knows it."

"Fine, fine. I'll keep it to myself. Let me see if I can guess what it was. You knew Einstein, U of T did research that may have been used for the A-Bomb, all the universities were doing research on atomic weapons. It's probably a reasonable bet that the backup plan was to drop the first A-bomb on Berlin, not Japan."

"No, the A-bomb was not ready in 1943 when the planning for D-Day began. Nor was it ready in 1944. It wasn't available until shortly after Germany surrendered in 1945. And when you asked if I just worked on the A-Bomb, I didn't say that it was the only thing. This plan did not involve atomic bombs. It was gas."

"Gas?" questioned Neville. "What kind of gas? Do you mean a toxic or nerve gas?"

"Exactly. Germany had been doing research on toxic gases for years. Gases like Tabun, Sarin and Soman. Germany was pretty good with gases. We know, now, how they tested and perfected them in the death camps. But using gases on the battle field is a much more complex problem than using them on captured victims in confined, controlled spaces."

"Because?" Neville questioned.

"The problem with gases is that they are not directional. If you release a gas, it doesn't just attack your enemy. It attacks in all directions. One of the difficulties Germany was having was developing an effective delivery method. You have to be able to deliver it into the midst of the enemy while they are not prepared. Clearly, if they have time to pull on their gas masks or protective equipment, the attack loses effectiveness. Also, what is the stability of the gaseous compound? Will it break down naturally and how quickly depending on the surrounding conditions? So you also have to consider the weather. Is the gas affected by humidity or rain, or even less predictable, the wind? How successful would a gas attack be if the wind caused it to douse your own troops? Hell, even recently, the US still had these kinds of chemical warfare problems with Agent Orange in Vietnam. They sprayed tons of that stuff and now we are seeing problems from exposures to their own troops."

"Your team of researchers found a way to deliver a gas as a battlefield weapon in 1944? Why didn't they use it to help land on the Normandy beaches?"

"Hmph, no," Doc Beege responded. "That's not quite the direction our research took. And it started in the fall of 1943..."

Doc Beege was gazing out the front window, watching the rain pour down beyond the cover of the bridge, as he began recalling his private history.

Chapter 3

The University of Toronto in the fall of 1943 had a world class chemistry department. With the infusion of government grants for war research, the facilities had been upgraded to be as good as those found at any university anywhere else in the world.

Dr. Ian Johnstone was Dean of Chemistry. He was fifty-eight, balding and a little overweight. He had been Dean for the last eight years now. Another two more years and he would turn the reigns over to someone else; perhaps someone already on his team. And he had a good team. The University had attracted some very talented professors, both as teachers and as researchers, and the Phd candidates and Master's degree candidates were plentiful and talented. Most notable in the department was a rising star - Dr. George Beege. That was not really a surprise; he was U of T from top to bottom. George had grown up in Toronto, done his undergraduate BSc at U of T, done his MSc at U of T, and then completed his PhD at U of T. He had been on staff at U of T for seven years now and had continuously confirmed to Ian that he had been an excellent choice to keep as a professor after graduation.

During the seven previous years, Dr. Beege had been assigned to a few corporate research contracts, and had come through those with shining stars. He would not become famous from these projects as his work was more behind the scenes. He wasn't like Edison developing the light bulb, but his inventions had been impressive to those in the know. He had been responsible for a chemical compound that improved the performance and durability of the heating elements of electric ovens and toasters. He also developed a chemical additive to glass that made it stronger, less likely to break. But now, his research was to benefit the allied forces. His research was enhancing the development of toxic gases that could be used on the battlefield.

He wasn't working alone. He had a team, a state-of-the-art laboratory and government financing. His team consisted of two more PhDs, Dr. Robert McQueen and Dr. Rick Van Dyke, and five PhD candidates: Steve Burton, Shawn Hatch, Daniel Davids, Donald Chan and Jeff Goorski.

Dr. Beege knocked on the office door of Dr. Johnstone. Ian looked up from the papers on his desk. "Oh, I'm sorry George, I completely forgot the time. Give me just a moment and we can have our status meeting." Ian quickly signed a few sheets of paper and pushed the pile to the side of the desk.

"Actually, why don't we grab some coffees on the roof?" Ian suggested as he rose from his desk.

"Sounds good to me," replied George as he turned and lead the way into the hallway.

The two men walked the hallway and went up the flight of stairs, talking as they went. "How are the little ones, George?"

"Neville just turned five last week. We had the grandparents, aunts, uncles, cousins all over for a BBQ last weekend. Twenty-five people crammed into our small back yard," George replied with a laugh. "Betty was in heaven. Nothing pleases a one year old more than being the center of attention of all the aunts."

They reached the roof. The chemistry building had been designed with a rooftop cafeteria. An enclosure covered the stairwell accesses and half of the roof. The inside of the enclosure had been configured as a café which served coffee, tea, soup, sandwiches and treats such as muffins and cookies.

Outside of the enclosure was a patio, with tables and chairs. Benches lined the edges along the brick parapet that secured the open area of the roof. On mild spring or fall days and hot summer days, people would come to the café for coffee and enjoy it out on the patio. The patio was attractive for two reasons. First, the rooftop patio offered a marvellous view of the campus, the surrounding city and Lake Ontario. Second, the patio was also home to the garden of Mrs. Margaret Richardson. Margaret ran the café, but spent all her spare time catering to the needs of dozens of potted plants and flowers that were on top of the parapet that surrounded the patio. She had been caring for these plants for as long as anyone could remember. Before the building had been remodelled, the café had been inside on the main floor, in the center of the building. Even in that location, the plants had flourished under the care of Mrs Richardson. The plants had been strong and healthy then, but when the café was moved upstairs and the outdoor patio opened, they flourished in the fresh air environment. Mrs. Richardson was known all over the campus as students and faculty from all disciplines had stopped into the café at one time or other over the years. It was often said in jest that Mrs. Richardson was a candidate to be the next chairperson of the botany department.

"Good morning Mrs. Richardson," said George with a smile. "Just a black coffee please."

"I'll have the same," added Ian.

"Coming right up," said Margaret. She was an older short, stocky lady, with gray hair that she almost always wore in a hair net.

"How's the garden doing? It looks like it is growing well," George asked as Margaret was pouring the cups of coffee.

"Yes, it has been a good year for the flowers. The hibiscus and asters are blossoming early this year. Just watch yourself if you sit near them. The bees have found the flowers already and have been particularly busy this fall."

The two men took their coffees from the counter after Ian passed Margaret a pair of quarters. They found a table in the middle of the patio where they could enjoy the warm morning sun and the view, but not be bothered by the bees.

"She wasn't lying about the bees," commented George as they sat.

"Huh?" grunted Ian.

"The bees. There's so many that you can hear them buzzing around the flowers."

"Oh yes, I guess you can. They are a busy lot, aren't they? Anyways, why don't you bring me up to date on your project?"

George sipped his coffee. "As you know, Robert, Steve, Shawn and Daniel are working on perfecting a long range delivery system for the gas. They've been experimenting with plastic formulas to develop a container that can be sealed air-tight and opened with a small explosive, small enough that the detonation would not affect the payload. They are getting close. They have a prototype now that could actually work if dropped from an airplane. They are trying to refine the design so that it can be small enough to use as a hand thrown weapon, like a grenade."

George continued, "The problem is that the gases tend to be unstable, reactive, so that they tend to eat through glass or plastics. Consequently, the gas has to be sealed within a wax container. Think of it like a wax balloon inside a plastic box. They are having a difficult time finding the right adjustments for the explosive and for the plastic formula; too strong, the explosive reaction ignites through the gas and renders it useless within seconds, too weak and the box breaks but the wax balloon stays intact. You would wind up with a very dangerous toy ball bouncing on the battlefield. The air drop version tends to eliminate that problem as the size and weight of the unit almost doesn't need the explosive. The ground impact from gravity typically breaks it apart."

"I can't imagine that the common infantry soldier would want to carry gas grenades. I think they'd be more afraid that an accident would occur before they were used," Ian commented.

"True, the average infantry soldier in the trenches wouldn't want it. But the specialty folks that often operate behind enemy lines can make good use of them. Consider the French Underground. They could use the gas grenades to cover escapes from their sabotage raids. The gas cloud could stop them from being pursued."

"Okay. Point made. It won't be very useful without a payload. How's that research coming?"

"Rick, Donny and Jeff have been working diligently on various fluorine gas formulas. It's very time consuming. The raw materials used in the mixtures are almost as dangerous as the final gas compound. Also, it's slow work.

They're working in the clean room and in the anti-gas suits. It literally takes a full day just to produce a hundred millilitres in the liquid form. Then they warm it to the gaseous form and test the toxicity against mice and rats. Rick and I have worked out a few formulas to test for ease of preparation, shelf life, storage, toxicity. Today's test formula should give a compound that should have a moderate solidify point and moderate vaporization point."

"And what do you consider moderate solidification and vaporizations points?" asked Ian.

"A low or moderate vaporization point will mean that the compound is gaseous at cooler temperatures. Gases may be ineffective in February, but the cooler requirements might have them effective in later March and November. And a moderate solidify point means that it stays as a solid to a higher temperature, meaning that it turns to a solid sooner and is easier to handle without requiring freezing. An ideal range would be something like solid below sixty degrees, gaseous above seventy degrees, and liquid in between."

"Excellent. Your team is doing good work. Keep me posted as to how it progresses. Also, I know a good, experienced mechanical engineering professor. Maybe he can assist with the delivery design," Ian said enthusiastically.

"Great. Send him to see Robert."

Robert was a young engineering PhD having just recently received his doctorate. His team consisted of Steve, a chemistry MSc graduate of UofT in his late twenties, Shawn, also in his late twenties, but a tall stocky Englishman with a chemistry MSc from Oxford, and Daniel, a small wiry mid-twenties biochemistry MSc from Western. George agreed that adding an experienced engineer to this group could only help the project.

The two men finished their coffees and returned the cups to Margaret. They wished her a good afternoon and went to their respective offices. Ian spent the rest of the afternoon authorizing departmental purchase requisitions.

George checked his calculations for the formula that was being tested today, then decided to drop into the laboratory to see how Rick and his helpers were progressing. The lab was located in the basement of the building. Below ground, with the heating turned off, the lab was typically about sixty-five degrees Fahrenheit, even in the summer. Keeping the temperature just right was important for the experiments being done as the mixtures were expected to need to be above eighty degrees to turn from liquid to gas. Although the room was ten to fifteen degrees cooler than necessary, that difference created a margin of safety.

George found Rick in his office which was located beside the lab. Rick was the youngest of the PhDs on the staff. He had gone to McGill University as an undergraduate and then to U of T for his MSc and PhD. He was tall and well built as he had been an athlete as well as a student, playing hockey for the McGill Redman and winning the Queen's cup four times during the early 1930s. After doing his MSc degree, he had been the first PhD candidate to have George as his PhD supervisor.

"This one's real tricky George," Rick said. "The zinc is very reactive with the other raw materials, so we're being extra careful in the mixture. I think we'll only be making between ten to twenty millilitres today."

"That's fine. It's getting late. Have the guys finish the mixture, store it and go home for dinner. We can test the toxicity tomorrow."

"Will do," replied Rick.

Chapter 4

George arrived home to find dinner already on the table. He was greeted by Neville, who was excited that his dad was home for the day. After dinner, George took Neville into the backyard to play and kick a ball around with Neville. Neville liked to kick the ball and then chase it. George would occasionally tap it, but thought it best to let Neville exhaust himself chasing the ball. Unfortunately, this evening's play was cut short as a fall rain came in.

"April showers bring May flowers," Neville had learned to say. He did not care that it was autumn instead of spring.

Back on campus, Donny and Jeff were the only ones in the chemistry building. Rick had asked them to finish the mixture and store it, and they agreed to do so before heading home.

Donny was third generation Canadian. He was a descendant of the Chinese that had come to North America and worked on the railways. He was tall and thin. He was not the most creative PhD candidate, but he worked hard and followed instructions meticulously.

Jeff was fairly stocky, perhaps a little overweight. Rick would describe him as 'the loud-mouth American'. Jeff did have a Bio-Chemistry MSc from Princeton, so in addition to being brass, he was also well-educated. While not being well liked, he was respected.

Jeff was monitoring the gauges and making notes as Donny delicately brought the raw materials together in stages. Each step was documented and the temperature of the test tubes monitored constantly. If a reaction was not proceeding as expected, there would likely be heat released, warming the tubes and the contents would go from liquids to vapours. As a safety precaution, the mixtures were all done using air-tight, wax lined containers so an errant mixture would be contained and neutralized with the addition of water. A water supply was always connected to the equipment so that the water could be added with the turn of a tap. They did all their work in the gas suits as well, for added protection.

"Right on schedule so far," said Donny. "Just this last step to add the zinc sub-mixture."

"So far so good," added Jeff.

"Okay, I'm opening the pipette now to let the zinc drip in. Keep your eye on the gauges."

"Got it," said Jeff.

Donny turned the tap just a little, releasing the zinc sub-mixture slowly into the base mixture.

"Flowing now," Donny said.

After a couple of seconds, Donny added, "This seems strange. The liquid measure does not appear to be going up. It's like everything is turning to gas as soon as it goes in."

"Are you sure?" asked Jeff. "It's only been a few drops. I don't think you should be able to notice a difference in the liquid level."

"Maybe. What's the temperature show?"

"Seems to be holding steady at sixty-five degrees," Jeff said looking at the gauge.

"I can see the zinc liquid level has clearly gone down now. But the base mixture has not increased in volume; in fact, it's gone down too. This stuff must be gaseous at sixty-five degrees. Rick did not expect that result. Make a note of it," said Donny.

"In a sec," said Jeff. "Let me just make sure this temperature gauge is working properly."

Jeff tapped it to see if the needle would wiggle. It did. Clearly, it was not stuck on sixty-five. Just to be sure, he put down his notepad and squeezed the gauge gently between his gloved hands. He checked after a few seconds and the temperature gauge had gone up a little from his body heat.

"Yup. The gauge is right," Jeff said.

"Good," said Donny, "because we're fully mixed now. And everything is gaseous. No liquid left in either tube."

"Okay, great. Transfer the gas to the flask and seal it so we can get out of here."

"Already on it," said Donny as he started the vacuum to suck the gas from the tube and expel it into the flask. It only took a few seconds.

"Done. Sealed." Donny disconnected the flask and set it on the desk. He did not notice that he sat the edge of the flask on Jeff's notepad.

Donny walked across the room and removed the headpiece of the gas suit. "Whew," he said, "these suits get hot after a while."

"Yeah," added Jeff. He had followed Donny across the room and was removing his headpiece as well. "I have a love-hate relationship with these suits. I love the protection, but I hate how uncomfortable they are."

"Agreed," laughed Donny. "Hey, did you make that note about the mixture turning to gas immediately at this temperature?"

"Oh, almost forgot," said Jeff. "I'll do that right now."

Jeff quickly crossed the room and grabbed his notepad, setting off a chain reaction that would prove to be fatal. The flask tipped on its side, and with its angular shape, rolled in a semi-circle away from Jeff and off the edge of the table. He reached to grab it, but in the suit, he was too slow and the flask hit the floor and broke open.

Both realized the situation immediately and reacted. Donny, furthest from the exit, tried to cross the room to get out the door. He only made it half way, started choking and hit the floor. The last thing he heard was the choking sounds of the cages full of lab animals.

Jeff, on the other hand, knew instantly that there was no escape and he quickly whirled and hit the alarm switch, engaging the emergency ventilation system. As he began to slide down the wall, choking, he tried to write that the mixture was gaseous at room temperature. '6 - 5 - G' was all he was able to write as he dropped the pen and coughed for the last time.

The laboratory alarm was ringing loudly. The fire department arrived on the scene first to find the building empty except for Jeff and Donny. The broken flask for the production of the gas mixture was on the floor by the desks. Donny was sprawled in the middle of the floor. It looked like he had been trying to get to the laboratory exit. Jeff was on the floor by the switch to the alarm, still holding his notepad. From his position, it was clear that Jeff had been the one to set off the alarm. His stockiness may have helped give him an extra few moments of life, enough to scribble a note saying '65 G'. Both Jeff and Donny were still wearing most of the gas suits, but they had both removed their headgear. The state of the art laboratory alarm system also launched the advanced ventilation system. Luckily, by the time the fire department had arrived, the laboratory had been fully vented.

Ian, George, and Rick were contacted and they all raced over to the building. An evening that had been so relaxing at home with family was not ending well. They waited just inside the front of the building, avoiding the rain, until the medical team had removed their two colleagues and the fire department had given the 'all clear'.

The three men met with the fire marshal, a tall man in the typical metal helmet, rubber coat and boots of the fire fighter. He had name tag that said Robinson, and he introduced himself as Wayne.

Wayne described how the scene inside had been found. "They were both dead on the floor. It looks like the big one had the fortitude to set off the alarm. They were both wearing strange suits, but the head pieces were sitting on the desk."

"Those are gas suits," George interjected. "They were working with toxic chemicals. If their head pieces were off, they must have had the mixtures completed and sealed in flasks."

"Well, there was also a broken flask on the floor. Strange too. The inside of the flask was coated with a waxy substance," replied Wayne.

"That is wax," added Rick. "The chemicals would eat through glass, so the inside of the flasks are coated with a layer of wax."

"Oh. Interesting," said Wayne. "So, what happened to the chemicals? The flask appeared to have been empty and we didn't seem to have been affected when we arrived."

"They must have warmed the flask so the contents turned into a gas. It would have to have been a gas to be lethal. The ventilation system would basically suck all the air and gas out of the laboratory. It would be vented through a charcoal filter to the outside. The filter should take care of the chemicals, and if a miniscule amount got past the filter, it would dissipate to safe levels outside within a short time."

"Well, it seems safe enough now for you folks to go inside. My men and I are ready to pack up and go," replied Wayne.

They started to go into the building, but Ian stopped suddenly and grabbed his colleagues by the arms. "Let's not go in yet. It's too early. We should all go home for the rest of the evening and try to unwind."

"That may be a good idea," added Rick.

"Right," added George. "Let's get here a little early in the morning, before the rest of the team arrives. We can catch them here at the door and break the news to them in an impromptu team meeting."

Rick and Ian agreed and they all left for the night.

At home, George could not sleep. He was trying to imagine what had happened. The fire marshal had told them that there was a broken flask. It seemed obvious that somehow the flask had been dropped and broken open, but the laboratory was cool and the mixture should have been in liquid form, unless they warmed it up. Since he had not gone inside, George did not know about Jeff's note. He finally fell asleep, but it was only a short time until he was up again and headed to the campus.

George was the first to arrive at the chemistry building. He sat on the steps and waited for the others to arrive. Ian and Rick both arrived shortly afterwards and the three of them sat on the steps in silence, waiting for the rest of George's team. Gradually the others trickled in, and they were asked to wait on the steps until everyone was there.

Once everyone had arrived, Ian addressed the group. "Last night, we had a very tragic accident here. Right now, we only have the information that the fire department has provided. From their description, we have surmised that Donny and Jeff had completed the mixture of the latest formula to be tested. With it sealed in the flask, they removed their head gear and we guess they were cleaning up to go. It seems that before they were able to safely store the mixture, the flask was damaged and broken. We guess that there must have been the gas in that flask and it overpowered both Donny and Jeff. Jeff appears to have reacted wisely and immediately set off the alarm. Despite Jeff's quick thinking, unfortunately, they were both killed."

Ian surveyed the devastated faces of his colleagues. "I think it is best if the rest of you take the day off. Unwind, relax, come back ready to work tomorrow. Today will not be productive."

Everyone stood in silence for a few moments. Nobody asked any questions. Then, as if on command, they all turned and headed away from the building, leaving Ian, Rick and George.

"Now, let's go into the laboratory and see if we can get a better idea of what happened," Ian said.

Chapter 5

Once inside the laboratory, the story of the night before came together fairly quickly, especially once they found the notepad.

"Six, five, G," said Ian, holding the notepad. "Do you think that means the mixture is gaseous at sixty-five degrees?"

"Yes, that's exactly what it means," responded George. "See where the flask is broken? There's no liquid there at all. The flask must have been completely gas and it's only about sixty-five degrees in here."

Rick took the notepad from Ian and flipped back through the notes. "According to their research notes, they were expecting to get about ten millilitres of the compound in liquid form. Everything proceeded as expected until the last step. The last note before the '65G' is that Jeff was checking the thermo gauge to see if it was operating properly. I think they were a little surprised that they were getting gas instead of liquid."

"While ten millilitres does not sound like much, it's more than enough to fill this room with gas at toxic concentrations," added George. "When the flask broke, this room would have been a death trap. It didn't take long to be effective either. Jeff must have hit the alarm almost right away."

"I think you're right," said Ian, walking towards the cages of the test rats and mice at the far end on the lab. "Have you noticed how quiet it is in here?"

"Not really," responded Rick. "Why?"

"All the animals are dead," said Ian calmly. "Either there was more gas created than they anticipated, or that gas is lethal even at low concentrations."

"Okay," Ian continued, "I think we have a grasp on what went wrong. It appears that the properties of the mixture were not exactly as expected, and clearly, our protocol should be to wear the entire gas suit until the flasks are safely stored."

"Why don't we go to the roof, grab coffees and discuss how to pick up and carry on?" George suggested.

The others nodded and they headed for the stairs. They made their way to the roof in silence. The events of the last twenty-four hours made small talk seem out of place.

When they reached the roof, they found Mrs Richardson busy making muffins in the café.

"Good morning Margaret," said Ian in a very subdued voice. "Can we get three coffees, please?"

Ian was reaching into his pocket for change, but Margaret stopped him. "These will be on the house. I already heard the news. Sad. Such young men."

The trio took their coffees over to the same table that George and Ian had used previously. Once seated, George looked around with a puzzled look on his face.

"What's wrong?" asked Ian.

"Too quiet," replied George.

"What are you talking about?" asked Rick.

"You're right," said Ian. "Yesterday when we were sitting right here, we could hear the bees buzzing around the flowers."

George got up and went to inspect the plants around the patio. When he got close, he noticed that the bees were there, but they were all dead. All the potted plants had dozens of dead bees around their bases.

"Margaret," George shouted towards the enclosure, "have you watered your flowers today?"

"No, I've been busy baking ever since I arrived," Margaret responded.

"I think you better come and look," George shouted back.

Margaret put down the muffin trays and made her way over to George, followed by Ian and Rick. She quickly noticed that the flowers were wilting.

"My poor flowers!" she exclaimed. "Something's wrong!"

Then she noticed the bees and looked puzzled at George.

"What happened to these bees? Do you know what's killing my plants?"

A terrible thought flashed through George's brain.

"Ian," George asked over his shoulder, "where does the laboratory vent go?"

"Someplace up here I think," Ian replied. "Why?"

"Ian, it appears that our gas is far more toxic than we expected. And it is appears that it is not limited to mammals. The bees and these plants must have been attacked by the gas being vented from the lab."

Chapter 6

The group returned to the table to finish their coffees. Margaret continued milling about the flowers, trying to determine if they were all damaged or if some could be saved. If anyone could help bring a dying plant back to life, it was Margaret.

"George, Rick, I think your immediate assignment is to get an understanding of this compound," said Ian.

"It was a very small amount of the mixture that they made last night, but that small amount was toxic to two humans, dozens of rats and mice, and then after being vented through a charcoal filter into open air, it was still lethal to hundreds of bees and a garden of flowers," summarized George. "As horrible as the last eighteen hours have been, this gas formula has already demonstrated having many of the characteristics we've been trying to achieve. We need to evaluate it carefully. It might be exactly what we have been trying to create."

"I think the 'evaluate it carefully' phrase is exactly right, with lots of emphasis on the 'carefully'. We don't want any more mishaps," added Rick mournfully.

"Here's what I think we should do. I don't want to bring any more doctoral candidates into the program unless we decide that this formula is wrong for our needs and we're back to square one. I want you two to finish the analysis of this formula. While you are doing that, I'll oversee the delivery team. I'm going to bring in that engineering help we discussed as soon as possible. Hopefully, by the time you two complete analysis of the formula, we'll have prototypes of the different delivery options," Ian directed.

Margaret finished her appraisal of the flowers. She came over to the group at the table.

"They're all dead or dying," said Margaret, referring to the plants. "Do you know why? Is it connected to the accident in the lab?" she asked.

"I'm afraid that it is," said George. "The boys were working with toxic chemicals in the lab and there was an accidental leak. Before they died, one of them set off the alarm and the ventilation system sucked the toxic air from the room. Apparently, the ventilation system exhausts the vented air near the roof. It appears that the vented gas killed the bees and the plants before it dissipated. I'm just thankful that you had left for the day already."

Margaret looked at him with a confused expression.

"If you had been on the patio last night when the alarm started, it would appear that the gas was toxic enough that you probably would not have made it out of the building. Also, if the ventilation system had not worked, there is a very good chance that some of the firemen could have been affected when they entered the lab."

"Oh, I never realized!" Margaret paused, "I was only a few minutes away from the building when the alarm started. I even considered coming back to see what was happening, but I didn't because I wanted to get home before the rain started."

"That rain may have saved your life. If it had not rained, there may have been enough of a toxic concentration of the gas still up here when you arrived this morning."

The group had finished their coffees. They thanked Margaret and headed for the stairs. George and Rick decided to return home for the rest of the day and dive into the research on the gas in the morning. Ian told them he would return to his office and contact his engineer friend before heading for home.

Ian made his way across the campus to the engineering buildings and the office of his friend Dr. John Starchek. John was an immigrant from Poland, but he had come with his parents when he was very young, so he spoke English perfectly, and Polish fluently. He was approaching his fortieth birthday but still kept himself in good shape by playing in the local men's recreational baseball leagues.

"Hello Ian. I'm quite surprised to see you today," John said. "Your tragic news has spread across campus like wildfire."

"That's exactly why I'm here," Ian replied. "The team needs help. We're now short a pair of researchers but it appears that they, unfortunately, demonstrated that we are on the right track for the development of a battlefield gas. However, we still need a delivery system to safely deploy the gas and that's where your expertise can be valuable. Can you work with the group that is responsible for the delivery system? They're lead by a young engineer and they already have some prototypes that they believe are close, but there are some mechanics that perhaps you can solve."

"When do you need me to start? I'm tied up for the next couple of days, but I could be there starting next week."

"Can you come over Monday? You can meet the team and get briefed on what they have accomplished."

"I'll be at your office by nine o'clock on Monday morning."

"Great. Welcome to the team," Ian said. They shook hands and Ian left for the day.

Chapter 7

The rest of the week was mercifully uneventful. George and Rick spent the time developing more samples of the mixture. As the compound's formula consisted of over ten chemicals, the name was too unwieldy for use in normal conversation. Since the main elements were fluorine and zinc, they had named the compound 'FluorZi'. They worked cautiously, knowing what had happened already with FluorZi, and always wore the complete gas suits while in the lab. Meanwhile, Robert and his team continued their work on a plastic-based delivery system and Ian had his secretary, Shelley, arrange for more test animals to replace the ones that had died in the accident.

At nine o'clock on the following Monday morning, John knocked on Ian's office door. Ian, George, Robert and Rick were already assembled and waiting for his arrival. After the introductions, it was quickly decided that the meeting should be moved to a more relaxing venue, and the group headed for the stairs.

On the roof, they got coffees from Margaret and sat down at their favourite table.

Before they had a chance to start their meeting, Margaret grabbed George's arm. "Come, I want to show you the new plants."

George followed Margaret over to her garden of potted flowers.

"I spent all Saturday taking out the old plants and planting these new ones in their place," she said. "Today, they all look unhealthy. I think they're dying too."

"When you changed the flowers, did you use the same soil?"

"There's some new soil, but a lot of the old soil is still there too."

"Interesting," said George. "I think you may have to do it all again. I think the soil may still be contaminated from before. Obviously, not lethal to people, otherwise we wouldn't be having this conversation, but it still won't support plant growth. I think you'll need to throw out these pots and use completely new soil. May I take one of these pots to the lab for analysis?"

"Absolutely. Take that one over there. I think its closest to where the lab vent is. At least, those flowers look to be the worst ones."

George took the suggested pot back to the table and sat it on the floor. Ian then gave a brief overview to John of the work being done. George and Rick described FluorZi, how it was gaseous at room temperatures, that it killed mammals, plants and insects, and how apparently, it contaminated soil against further plant growth. Robert updated the group on the work they were doing towards a battlefield hand delivery system.

The meeting adjourned. Ian returned to his office and paperwork, George and Rick returned to the laboratory to continue the study of FluorZi, and Robert and John went to meet the rest of Robert's team.

Weeks passed. George and Rick spent much of the time testing the properties of FluorZi and refining the production process, always wearing the complete gas suits until everything was cleaned up and put away. Robert and John experimented with different designs for delivery casings. Margaret brought life back to the patio with new plants. The bees returned in force until the temperatures became too cold on the outdoor patio. As the temperatures cooled, the meetings moved from the patio to the tables inside the rooftop enclosure. Finally, in mid November, a full team meeting was convened.

George opened the meeting with a summary of their research on FluorZi. He began by listing the characteristics. "FluorZi is extremely toxic. A small amount in the atmosphere is lethal to all life, animal or plant. And standard gas masks are not adequate protection. The gas can be absorbed through the skin and kill without it having entered the lungs.

"FluorZi changes from solid to liquid at forty-seven degrees and from liquid to gas at fifty-five degrees. For three seasons of the year, FluorZi would exist almost exclusively as gas.

"FluorZi is a fairly stable compound. It does break down reasonably quickly in the damp moving air of a rain storm, it does react with water to break down into other compounds and it will break apart in extreme heat; otherwise, it has a fairly long span in the atmosphere before any natural decomposition occurs. And when it's absorbed into the soil, it remains lethal to plants for weeks or longer. It was only a miniscule amount that was first created and vented out of the laboratory, but the contaminated soil from the pot I took from the rooftop patio tested positive for the presence of FluorZi for several weeks afterwards. It appears that it attacks even the microbes in the soil.

"In summary, our research shows that FluorZi is far too dangerous to be used as a battlefield gas. Even under the best, most controlled conditions, the gas spreads way too fast and is far too toxic for the soldiers to work with or use in battle. It could be used effectively in air assaults, and a small bomb dropped from a plane could cause devastating casualties," concluded George.

"That's actually good for us," added Robert. "We're still having difficulty with the design for a hand-thrown weapon, so taking that option off the table won't bother us at all."

"Just exactly how dangerous and toxic is this gas?" asked Ian.

"Let me put it this way. If I took a gallon of the liquid form to the top of a mountain in British Columbia and exposed it to a Chinook wind, the eastward wind would carry across the Prairies, killing every person, animal, insect and plant in Alberta and Saskatchewan, and nothing would grow there for four or five years afterwards."

"Wow," commented Ian. "I guess that use from an airplane would also be extremely dangerous. I assume that a bomb dropped with a significant amount of gas could devastate a small city. But what if the plane crashed before reaching the target?"

"Wherever that plane came down," replied George, "would be destroyed, uninhabitable for a long while. That risk alone might make it too dangerous for the air force."

"Oh great," said Ian disappointedly. "We've developed the world's most deadly gas for the military to use and it's too potent for military use. What do we do with it now?"

"I think John has the answer," interjected Robert. "John, tell them about the mid-level design you have."

John took the floor. "We think we have a design that can be used by the underground. We construct a pyramid shaped container, a flat base and four triangular sides that meet at the top. Inside the pyramid, we place a ball of wax containing the gas. In fact, the plastic can be shaped so that the inside is solid around the ball of wax, that will help stabilize it and keep it from being broken if shaken during transportation. In the top point of the pyramid there is a smaller pyramid, so the base of it protects the top of the wax ball. The base of this smaller pyramid has a center hole. Inside this small pyramid is a small charge and a plunger. When a fuse is lit, it burns down, ignites the charge, drives the plunger through the wax and releases the gas. The charge is just enough to drive the plunger into the wax, so it has already burned out by the time the gas emerges. We propose to use magnesium fuses, similar to current hand grenades, so that the fuse will also burn underwater or in damp environments. The fuse can be coiled in the top smaller pyramid so that a long duration can be accomplished. Inside the top pyramid, the burning will be more concealed. We can get a long burn time, perhaps as long as an hour."

"So, you're proposing that the underground can perform a sabotage raid, then leave one of these pyramids behind with a long enough fuse to allow them to get away?"

"Yes, or even use the pyramid as the instrument of the attack. If it could be detonated near a military facility, the whole facility could be wiped out or significantly damaged. Our prototype can hold a 250 millilitre payload and is only ten inches tall on an eight-inch by eight-inch base. It can be buried so that only the top is at surface level, making it very easy to conceal. Also, we plan to glue the plastic closed once the payload is in place, that way, anyone that tries to break it open to stop the fuse will almost assuredly break open the wax container, releasing the payload. The top pyramid will still be open to allow the fuse length to be customized."

"Excellent," said Ian. "Do we have to do any more research with the gas?"

"No," said George. "We've even improved the production method as well. We could safely make about one litre per week in the lab now."

"Good," Ian said, nodding his head. "I'm going to send the report of our progress to the war department. I suggest we all take a few days off, have a long weekend, and then starting on Monday, work together over the next few weeks to finalize the design of the pyramid."

The idea of the long weekend was passed without complaint.

Chapter 8

Ian took the following days off just like the team. He drove north to Lake Muskoka with his dog Duke, a large but gentle German Shepherd. He knew of a scout camp located on a quiet bay near the villages of Bala and Torrance. He spent the days fishing from a canoe for bass and trout, reading a Sherlock Holmes mystery and playing with Duke. The fall days were brisk, but the fish were biting and he had no trouble catching dinner for himself and Duke for a few days. It was a little chilly at night, but the camp fire outside the tent threw off enough heat to keep him warm and kept the bears and wolves away from the scent of the fresh caught fish.

The racoons, on the other hand, were more mischievous. One night, he left a live trout in the shallows on a stringer, planning to have it fresh for breakfast, but in the morning, he found it on the shore with several bites taken from it. It was a well enjoyed breakfast - just not by him. On the Sunday evening, he drove back to Toronto.

Monday morning, Ian went to the office and penned his report to the Government War Department in Ottawa. The report covered the characteristics of FluorZi and specified the conditions in which it was believed it could be deployed. The report also described the pyramid designed delivery system, including specifications for the plastic shell. Because Ian believed that FluorZi was the most toxic, dangerous man-made gas ever discovered, he wisely decided to keep the chemical formula out of the report.

The report was received and sat in the in-basket of a mid-level clerk, along with the other reports from a variety of institutions and corporations. Within a week, however, the report was reviewed by that mid-level clerk and was quickly escalated through his supervisor, department head, division leader and finally into the hands of a senior government official.

The senior government official quickly recognized the value of what he was reading. He arranged for copies to be made and within a few days, the copies had been distributed to all the military advisors and government war committee members. Within a week of his receipt of the report, a sub-committee had been formed to do a detailed review of the report and provide recommendations.

By mid-December, a meeting of the government war committee and military advisors was held. The sub-committee lead the meeting and reported their findings, recommendations and additional options. The recommendations and options were discussed and debated, and finally a consensus was reached.

"So, now that we have a plan that we believe has a very reasonable chance of successful execution, what do we tell Churchill?" the meeting chairperson inquired.

"I think," replied one of the military advisors, "that we should just tell him enough to keep England from trying to alter it or take credit for it."

"I agree," said another official, "but I think they will not pay much attention to it anyway. At the moment, they are occupied with other activities."

Further discussion followed and the details to be provided to England and the USA were debated, voted and finalized.

"Finally," said the chair, "we need someone to spearhead making the arrangements for the military personnel and transportation."

"I can take care of that," one of the military advisors replied.

With that, the meeting was adjourned and the government committee went back to their offices to look at more reports, and the military advisors went off to begin the arrangements for executing the plan.

Three military advisors took responsibility for the phases of the operation. One advisor would arrange for the Canadian Forces personnel and relay the plan to the European underground forces. The second would arrange for transportation, including a submarine from the US Navy. The third would work with Dr. Ian Johnstone's team to get the required product ready.

On Friday, the 24th of December, Ian's team was having a very relaxed afternoon since it was Christmas Eve. There were even a few drinks being shared amongst the team. The main topic of conversation was that it had been about a month since Ian had submitted his report and they had not heard anything from the powers that be. So, it wasn't a complete surprise when the courier package arrived in the middle of their party. What was a surprise, however, was that the courier was not a civilian, but two armed Canadian Forces Military Police soldiers.

Ian accepted the package from the soldiers and signed a receipt for it. He opened it and skimmed through the details. The response from the government was fairly short. They were to make a hundred units of the 250 millilitre pyramids, each having the maximum length of fuse time that could be contained within the inner pyramid. There were instructions that the units needed to be completed by the middle of April and that they were to be transported for use by the European underground, just as his report had recommended. There was also an instruction that at least one of Ian's team was to travel with the product to provide training to the European underground. Ian decided quickly that he would keep that last point to himself until after Christmas as there was no point in ruining a family's holiday by telling them that their loved one would be going on a very dangerous trip.

"Okay, okay," Ian said to the group. "There's good news and bad news here. The good news first, they want a hundred pyramid units. The bad news," he paused and looked around the room, "they want them completed by mid-April so they can be delivered to the European underground by June."

There was a cheer for the good news which drowned out the bad news enough that it didn't register with anyone initially. But as the cheer died down ....

"Mid-April? hmm... that could pose a problem," George said. "A hundred units would be twenty-five litres, five gallons! We can only make about one litre per week at the moment. Unless we ramp-up our processes, we won't be able to meet that deadline. It only gives us about fifteen weeks from now! And we probably need two weeks to make final assemblies of a hundred units. We'd need to double our production rates to make this deadline."

"That problem," said Ian, "is one that we can think about through this Christmas weekend and brainstorm a solution on Monday. We'll have a full team meeting Monday morning at ten o'clock. Have a merry Christmas everyone."

Chapter 9

Major General Darren Reed was also enjoying the afternoon of December 24th, 1943. He was the commanding officer of STS-103, also known as Camp-X, the paramilitary training camp on the north shore of Lake Ontario, a short distance east of Toronto. Even though the camp specialized in training commandos and paratroopers, the camp did not appear to be such a formidable place, at least not today. The men had been given the day off from training and had spent the day decorating the inside and outside of their barracks. There had been a lot of effort put into the decorations as there was a contest between the barracks to be the best decorated. The prize of the contest was an extra day off of training for the winning barracks. Darren was to be the judge.

Darren was in his office, attempting to work at a very casual pace, but he was spending more time staring out the window at the activities of the trainees below. With his office in the corner of the top floor of the main building, he had a bird's eye view of the efforts of the trainees, the snowball fights that were happening between the barracks teams, and the sneaky efforts of each team as they tried to sabotage their opponents' decorations. He smiled to himself watching world class saboteurs attempt to guard against and outwit each other. As valuable as the prize was, the interactions between teams were all of a friendly nature, for no team dared to be truly underhanded or violent and risk being disqualified from the competition.

The prize was valuable to the trainees because no one was allowed to leave the camp. Once you arrived at Camp X, you were there until you completed training and then you were sent off to Europe to create havoc behind the enemy lines.

Consequently, the training was comprehensive, covering the use of all sorts of weapons, hand-to-hand combat, operation of tanks and other vehicles, explosives, camouflage, wilderness survival techniques and anything else that they would need to know to survive behind enemy lines. The trainees were all hand selected and were truly the best of the best soldiers available from Canada and the USA. The training was also every day, year round with only one exception: Christmas Day. Although Christmas Eve was also like a day off with no formal training, whether the trainees realized it or not, their training was being tested in a playful manner. The decorating competition would give a Boxing Day holiday to the winners.

Apart from Darren, the only other people truly working were the office administrative staff; the cooks who were preparing a camp wide feast; and the senior training officers. The senior training officers were exempt from the decorating contest for two reasons. First, they had to lead the training on Boxing Day for all the barracks that did not win the contest, so their jobs prevented them from having the additional day off. Secondly, they were not assigned to trainee barracks. They had their own barracks, so if they entered the contest, they would be their own team. Darren had ruled them ineligible for the contest because he knew that, as camp graduates and fully trained commandos, they would be the most devious and mischievous saboteurs in the contest, clearly unfair to all the trainees.

From his window, Darren could also see the main gate, so he watched as a Canadian Forces Military Police vehicle approached and entered the compound. He noticed that the vehicle contained two officers. He watched the vehicle come over to the command center and he waited with curiosity for the two visitors to be escorted to his office. It was very unusual for CFMPs to be at the camp. The quality of trainees at the camp typically meant that CFMPs would not be needed. The training was too constant and intense for the trainees to have enough free time to be involved in any activity that would attract the attention of the CFMPs.

The two CFMPs were directed into the Major General's office, came to attention and saluted. Darren returned their salute.

"At ease," Darren instructed, and the two moved to stand easy positions. "What can I do for you today, gentleman?"

"Sir, we have a package for Major General Reed, Sir," responded one of the CFMPs.

"I'm Major General Reed," replied Darren. "See, it says so on the name plates on my door and my desk," he added with a bit of Christmas cheer. The CFMPs did not smile.

"Oh, lighten up. It's Christmas Eve," Darren chided, as he took the package from the CFMP.

"Sir, please sign for the package, Sir," said the second CFMP as he presented a clipboard with a receipt to be signed.

Darren took the clipboard, signed, and handed it back.

"Is that everything?" asked Darren.

"Sir, yes, Sir," replied the CFMPs in unison.

"Dismissed," said Darren.

The CFMPs snapped to attention, saluted, turned and walked out of the office.

"Merry Christmas!" called Darren after them.

"Merry Christmas to you too, Sir," one of them replied over his shoulder as they continued to walk out.

Darren watched them drive out of the camp before opening the package.

The package contained just a few sheets of paper, plus a sealed envelope. The document instructed Darren to select a "Volunteer" to report to Dr. Ian Johnstone, Chemistry Department at the University of Toronto and assist as directed by Dr. Johnstone with the final preparation of a new weapon to be delivered to the underground forces in North Germany. The volunteer was to select a team to assist with the transportation of the weapon from Toronto to Halifax; from there, the weapon would be transported via submarine to North Germany. The volunteer would also be responsible for the safe transportation of the weapon and one or two professors who would accompany the weapon to North Germany. Once inside North Germany, the volunteer would turn the weapon over to the underground forces and assist the professor(s) with the training of the underground forces in the handling and deployment of the new weapon. As soon as the weapon was in the hands of the underground and training complete, the volunteer would ensure the safe return, via submarine, of the university professor(s). Additionally, the volunteer would carry the sealed envelope of additional orders, to be opened upon arrival in North Germany. The additional orders were to be destroyed, unopened, if there was any possibility that they should fall into enemy hands.

Darren filed the document away, put the envelope neatly into the inside pocket of his uniform jacket and went out of his office. He went down the hallway to the stairs, down one level and down the hall to the office of Captain Tom Wallace. Tom was the senior trainer at the camp, and he was proficient in almost every discipline. He had already led two successful missions behind enemy lines with teams of graduates from the camp.

"Stay at ease," Darren said as he walked, unannounced, into Tom's office and closed the door.

Tom was at his desk working on the lesson plan for Boxing Day, and he looked up as Darren came in.

Darren looked around the office like he was taking measure of the room.

"Are you claustrophobic?" Darren asked with a smile. Compared to Darren's office, Tom's office was much smaller, but in relation to the other trainers' offices on the same floor of the building, it was about the same size.

"Not that I am aware, Sir. This office is not so small that it would cause a claustrophobic reaction," Tom replied. Then he added with a smile, "Of course, if I was claustrophobic and if that would require that I trade offices with someone upstairs, then I am extremely claustrophobic, Sir."

"There is only one office upstairs," Darren replied.

"I'm sorry to displace you, Sir," said Tom, holding back a laugh, "but I did not design the building."

Darren stared at him for a moment, then broke into laughter, prompting Tom to do the same. Darren and Tom had been together in the camp since it opened. While there was a difference in their ranks, behind closed doors they were more like brothers and all formality associated with their ranks was forgotten.

When the laughing stopped, Tom turned to Darren. "I'm sure you didn't come down here to discuss office sizes."

"No," said Darren. "I've been tasked with finding a volunteer to accompany the delivery of a new weapon from the University of Toronto to the European underground forces.

It will involve travelling from Halifax to North Germany in a submarine. Hence, the concern about claustrophobia."

"Interesting," said Tom. "We have several trainees that are close to graduation and any one of them would be up to the task, not to mention any of the other trainers."

"No," said Darren. "Under normal circumstances, I would agree with your comment but there is an extra wrinkle with this mission. There is a sealed order that is not to be opened until arrival in Germany. I have a suspicion that the sealed order is of paramount importance and should not be left up to a recent graduate. And, the instructions that I received were delivered by CFMPs from the Office of the Prime Minister. That is very unusual. The content must be extremely delicate otherwise, like most orders, it would have come via telegraph or courier. Not one, but two armed CFMPs were assigned to deliver it. The delivery envelope was not made of gold, so the content must be valuable. And the content of the document that I read was not all that enlightening, so the value must be in the sealed envelope. I can only imagine whose signature is inside that envelope, but I'm sure it's likely near, if not at, the top."

Tom waited for Darren to continue as Darren paused for a moment to allow the information to sink in.

"I was thinking that I would volunteer you," Darren added.

"I'll make it easy for you. I volunteer," Tom replied. "This will not be my first adventure to Europe but I've never been to North Germany, and I've always wanted to ride in a submarine."

Darren gave Tom the additional details from the package and handed the sealed envelope to him.

"I'll have my secretary make arrangements for you to stay in Toronto."

"No need," replied Tom. "My sister lives near the university. Her husband was a casualty overseas, so I'm sure she has room and will be glad to see me for a few weeks."

"Good," Darren said with a nod. "You should report to Dr. Johnstone on Monday."

Chapter 10

Ian arrived at his office on Monday, December 27th, at nine o'clock in the morning, an hour before the scheduled team meeting. Upon arrival, he found a uniformed man sitting in the guest chair outside of his office. The man was clean shaven and big, easily over six feet and three inches and he looked like he could scale the outside of building with his bare hands without breaking a sweat.

"Can I help you?" Ian asked as he walked into his office.

"Are you Dr. Ian Johnstone?" came the reply, as Tom followed him into the office.

"Yes," said Ian, signalling Tom to sit in the guest chair.

"I'm Captain Wallace. I've been assigned to assist with the delivery of your new weapon to the European Underground forces in North Germany. I assume you've received similar instructions."

"I think you're a little early," replied Ian. "We just received the order for the weapon on Friday. We still have to make it. At the moment, there are only prototypes. We won't be ready to ship it for another three months."

"I am aware of that timetable," said Tom. "My orders are to participate in the final production under your direction. I believe that the intent is that I gain some familiarity with the unit prior to transporting it. I am also aware that I am to guard one or two professors who will accompany the weapon to North Germany and bring them home safely."

"That last point," said Ian, "is a secret between you and I. I have not decided who should go so I have not even mentioned that part of the order to anyone. Please don't mention it and until we determine who will be travelling, and please keep that in mind when answering any questions about transportation. The team is aware that there will be people joining us to assist with transportation when the product is ready, but they will be mildly surprised to find you here already. I'm sure there will be friendly curiosity and questions over the next few weeks."

"I will try to make sure I don't let it slip," said Tom.

"Okay. We have a full team meeting at ten o'clock. Perhaps you could wait outside while I get organized and then you can accompany me to the meeting and meet the team. Since you're here already, we'll put you to use."

"Sure Dr. Johnstone," Tom said. "I'll wait in the outer office."

"Ian. Call me Ian. We're a small team and generally very informal. We all just use first names. I hope you don't mind, Tom."

"Sure Ian," replied Tom. "First names are fine by me."

Tom turned and went into the outer office and waited. Ian's secretary, Shelley, was just arriving and Tom introduced himself, as 'Tom'.

Ian watched through the door as Tom shook hands with the secretary. "I hope you don't mind..." he thought to himself sarcastically. "If he minded, he could probably just tear my head off," he chuckled to himself.

Ian prepared himself for the meeting. He had the order he had received ready to take to the meeting in case he needed to refer to it. As ten o'clock approached, he got up, corralled Tom and headed to the meeting place. The meeting, as had become the custom, was held in the rooftop café.

Ian bought coffee for himself and Tom. He introduced Tom to Margaret. They grouped some tables together to have enough seats for the meeting and sat and waited for the others to arrive. As they came in, Ian introduced them to Tom.

John and George strolled in together, grabbing coffees as they made their way to the table. They were the last to arrive. "And this is Dr. John Starchek and Dr. George Beege," said Ian. "John is the engineer who designed the gas delivery system. George created the gas formula with Rick. John, George, this is Captain Tom Wallace. It would appear that the military involvement has started already. Tom is starting with our team today."

"Welcome to the team," said George. "Where did you find a military representative already?" George asked Ian.

"Actually, he found us. He was waiting for me at my office when I arrived this morning," replied Ian. "I forgot to ask if you had been waiting long," Ian said to Tom.

"I wasn't told what time you started in the morning, so I came early and waited," Tom replied.

"So, you were outside my office since eight o'clock?" Ian asked.

"Six," was the reply.

"The building isn't open at six. I think the maintenance staff open it about eight," said George.

"I'm aware of that now," Tom laughed. "I waited outside until the maintenance staff opened it at five past eight."

"What time do you usually work each day?" asked John.

"Six-to-six most days," said Tom.

"Well," said George with a chuckle, "you're going to feel like you're on vacation with us. We usually just work nine-to-five."

"Before we start, perhaps you can fill us in on your background, Tom," Ian suggested.

"I'm a training officer at STS-103," Tom started. "I've been in the army for almost twenty years now. Explosives, marksmanship and survival training are my specific areas of expertise. I've been assigned to your team as of last Friday to assist with the final assembly of a new weapon and its transportation to Europe. And, until two minutes ago, I did not know that the new weapon is a gas weapon."

"Have you been to Europe before?" asked Robert.

"Yes."

Robert waited for Tom to elaborate. When it was obvious he was not going to, he asked, "Where?"

"I can't say. It's classified," replied Tom.

"Classified?" asked Daniel, with a bit of a smirk. "Why? Did you kill someone?" Daniel, who often considered himself to be the group's master of comedy, inquired.

"Yes," said Tom remaining totally expressionless. Then after a few moments of silence, "With my bare hands," he added with a wink towards Daniel.

"You say that as a joke," said Ian, "yet somehow, I think it might actually be true." Ian was reminded about his earlier thought when he first met Tom.

Tom toasted his coffee cup towards Ian.

"Okay Tom," said George, "here's where we are. We have developed the most toxic gas known to date. It has already accidentally claimed the lives of two of our teammates, dozens of laboratory animals and a garden full of plants. We've determined that it is too toxic to be safe to use for air attacks as an accident could wipe out an entire airfield, and it's too toxic for use in weapons deployed in close quarters like a hand grenade because it spreads too fast and is lethal for too long. But, we believe that it can be used where the gas cloud is created after our forces are clear, like used by the underground. John has designed a container which releases the gas using an ignition system like a grenade. That's the information that we provided to the war committee. Last Friday, we were informed that they want a hundred of these units to be in the hands of the underground for next June. And today, you've arrived. Now our immediate problem is to determine how to make a hundred units for June, since our current production rate only allows for fifty in that time frame. The purpose of today's meeting is to determine how to double our production rate."

"What we need," said Robert, "is a second lab. Then we could do productions in both laboratories. Maybe we can convert some offices into a second laboratory?"

"No," George said firmly. "We can't use a room that does not have the proper safety equipment. I think we're stuck with using just the laboratory. What we need to do is to arrange the lab so that we have room for two production work streams."

"We can make some more room by moving out the lab animals," Steve said.

"Maybe we can convert an office into a room for the animal cages," Shawn suggested.

"I think that can be arranged," said Ian. "I'll get Shelley to work on it. We also have to arrange to move the vent away from the roof. It's too risky to stay there if we're going to be making large quantities. Imagine if there were people on the patio when the accident occurred."

"I don't think there is any safe place for the vent to be exhausted," said John, "but the gas is neutralized in water, right?"

"Right," replied Rick, "or in extreme heat."

"Then I'll extend the vent via a hose into a fifty gallon drum. We'll put the lid on the drum and fill it with water, just leaving a small hole in the lid open. If the vent system is activated, the gas will be passed through the drum of water. That should neutralize it."

"Okay," said Ian. "Set it up, but take a small amount of the gas we have already and release it in the lab and run the vent system. Capture an air sample as it comes out through the drum. Shawn and Steve will assist you. Make sure the whole patio is cleared before you conduct the test. Notify the fire department so they don't respond to the alarm."

"Notify the fire department that they have to come," said George. "They're the only ones authorized to turn off the alarm. Have them be here before you set off the alarm so they can turn it off right away."

"Fine," said Ian. "And gas suits worn by everyone during the test."

"Tom, you'll have to vacate during the test. We don't have a gas suit that you could fit into," laughed Daniel.

"Actually, that's a good point," said Ian seriously. "I'll have Shelley arrange for a larger gas suit too."

Chapter 11

Shelley arranged for the maintenance staff to empty out a storage space in the basement. As much as Ian thought it was a good idea to empty out an office to make room for the laboratory animals, there were no offices available on the upper floors. On top of that, Shelley knew there would be two problems with having the lab animals closer to the rest of the chemistry department. Firstly, some people might have allergies and would be affected by the proximity to the animals. Secondly, even though the guys took good care of the animals, until they were the test victims, the animals still, quite frankly, stank. Shelley managed to find a storage area in the basement that could be cleared so the animals could be moved there.

Daniel, Steve and Shawn moved the animals and their cages into the storage area once it was empty. At one point, Daniel was alone in the lab while Steve and Shawn were stacking cages in the new room. He pulled out two rabbits and set them loose in the hall. "Hey! Stop! Come back!" he yelled which drew Steve and Shawn into the hall. Then Daniel sat back, unseen, and laughed watching the other two try to get their hands on the quick moving rabbits. Eventually, they corned the two rabbits and picked them up. Daniel came down the hall carrying the empty cage.

"I think you did that on purpose," huffed and puffed Shawn as they secured the rabbits back into the cage.

"Oh no," said Daniel. "They're smart little guys. We need to keep a close eye on them or they'll get out again."

"Nonsense," wheezed Steve, "but I'll put their cage at the top of the pile, just in case."

They finished moving the animals to the storage room. Steve and Shawn made sure that one of them was always with Daniel and no other animals escaped. They re-arranged the tables and equipment in the lab, making room for eight people to make two FluorZi production lines.

Tom assisted John with setting up the water filter for the ventilation system. John thought to himself that getting the fifty gallon drum onto the roof, with Tom's help, was easy. In reality, it was easy because Tom pretty much carried it all by himself up the five levels of stairs. Once it was there, they brought up a roll of fire hose and Tom, fastening himself in place with a rope, nimbly went over the side of the building and attached the hose to the end of the ventilation system.

"It seems you've done this before," said John commenting on Tom's familiarity with ropes and the way he swung down to the end of the vent.

"Well, not exactly. My training covers scaling walls and cliffs with full gear packs on our backs, but I've never had to manipulate equipment in the middle of the climb. Usually we try to spend as little time on the rope as possible. Up quick, down quick. Stopping along the way can get you killed," replied Tom as he tightened the connection with a wrench. To prove his point, he was back on the roof in just a few seconds.

The other end of the hose was passed through a hole in the lid and fastened in place. Then using buckets, John and Tom carried water from the tap in the kitchen in the café over to the drum and dumped them in. Actually, John filled the buckets while Tom carried them and filled the drum.

At the end of the day, Shawn and Steve affixed a collection unit onto the lid of the rooftop drum. It would catch everything that bubbled out of the water in the drum when the ventilation system was activated. Then they waited for the building to be completely empty. They called the fire department and waited for them to come. Once all was set, they dawned their gas suits, activated the alarm and ventilation system and released a full 250 millilitre load directly into the intake vent.

They took air samples from the intake vent while the fire department deactivated the alarm. Afterwards, they went to the roof and drew air samples from the collection unit at the drum. They returned to the lab and tested the samples for FluorZi. As expected, the samples from the intake vent were clear, indicating that the ventilation system had worked. The samples from the collection unit on the water drum were also clear. John's system had worked perfectly. FluorZi was neutralized when forced to pass through the water.

It took an extra day for the additional supplies and equipment to be delivered, including gas suits for both John and Tom. While waiting, John dissected one of the prototype pyramids so that Tom could understand the mechanics. Tom, being an expert in military explosives, was quite impressed with the spindle system that John had invented to wind the fuse in such a way that in did not contact itself partway and shorten the burn time. While John was bringing Tom up to speed on the pyramid, the rest of the team started production of the twenty-five litres of FluorZi that would be required for the hundred pyramids ordered, using the equipment already on hand.

The first thing they did was to break into two production teams. George suggested Robert and Rick lead one team, and he would lead the other. Then George produced a deck of cards and drew out three jacks.

"The jack of spades is Shawn, the jack of clubs is Steve, and the jack of diamonds is Daniel," George said as he mixed the cards around in his hand. Then he spread them and said to Rick, "Go ahead, Pick one." Unfortunately for Rick, he had no idea that George had always been fascinated with magicians in his youth and had mastered some sleight of hand tricks with cards. Consequently, it was not a surprise to George that Rick chose the red card; Rick really didn't have a choice.

"Since you have drawn Daniel," George said, "I'll let you also have John and I'll take Tom." Rick and Robert agreed, although Rick had a suspicious feeling that the teams had been pre-determined.

With the passing of another day, the new equipment and gas suits had arrived. They spent December 30th and half of the 31st working as two distinct production lines. Shawn, Steve and Daniel, all being chemists, were already familiar with the production process. Robert, John and Tom were all quick learners and by lunchtime on the 31st, they had their roles down perfectly. Robert and John, as engineers, had done some chemistry work as undergraduates. Tom, as an explosives expert, was actually more proficient with the chemicals than Robert and John.

When they broke for lunch, Ian had ordered a catered meal as a year-end celebration. They all met on the rooftop patio.

"Is anyone making new year resolutions?" Ian asked.

Most of them did not have an answer. Tom piped up, "I resolve to make the mission to Europe successful and return safely."

"What would you be doing if you weren't assigned to this project?" asked Daniel.

"Right now? I'd be celebrating the new year with the trainees and instructors at the camp."

"Don't they get to go home for New Year's Eve?" asked Steve.

"No," replied Tom. "The people at the camp are from all over. Only one or two could get home and back if they were given time off. One thing about the army, they don't group people based on their geography. They make teams of a variety of skills, regardless of where they're from. So, to be fair to those that are from far away, they do not get any days off, except Christmas and perhaps this afternoon."

"What about family?" asked Ian. "Do you have any?"

"Just my sister. I'm staying with her," said Tom.

"Bring her tonight," Ian suggested.

"To?" asked Tom.

"Don't you know? The university is hosting a faculty New Year's Eve party," replied Ian.

"I know, but I'm not faculty," said Tom.

"You're working with us. That makes you part of the staff here as far as I'm concerned. I'm sorry, but I should have told you about the party before today. I hope you don't have other plans," Ian said.

"Yes, you're one of us now. If anyone asks, we'll say you have a master's degree in military mayhem," Daniel joked, and they all joined in with laughter.

Chapter 12

The New Year's Eve party was held in the university arena. The ice had not been in the arena since the beginning of the war. Consequently, U of T held the title of Intercollegiate Hockey Champions for the last three years without having to defend it as the university hockey competitions had been suspended. U of T and McGill University had been the only two teams to win the Queen's Cup since the end of WWI, with U of T winning the latest one in 1940.

The arena floor was set up with tables and chairs for the guests, a bar and a light buffet, occupying the area from one end zone to the far blue line. The other end zone was a dance floor and a brass band was providing the entertainment.

Most of the team had come out for the party. Ian was there with his wife, and John, the bachelor that he was, came alone. The younger guys, Shawn and Steve were accompanied by their girlfriends, both of them being M.Sc. students in other disciplines. Everyone was surprised when Daniel arrived with a date. Being the group smart-ass, everyone believed that most girls would not be able to tolerate him, but there was something different about this girl from the rest of the dates that the group had brought. She was obviously not a graduate student, and Shawn and Steve remarked to each other that she seemed barely out of high school. Yet, around her, Daniel was like another person, a true gentleman, much more quiet and subdued. Clearly, she had some magic spell on him.

Notably absent were George, Rick and Robert. George and Robert had young families and opted to spend the night at home. Rick mentioned in the afternoon that he was feeling a little exhausted and would stay home to relax.

Tom arrived single as well, except he was accompanied by a beautiful lady that he introduced as his younger sister, Lily. John was immediately smitten.

Lily was several years younger than Tom. Everyone was too polite to ask her age, but the consensus was that she was twenty-eight or twenty-nine. She was a nurse at the Toronto General Hospital and had been a war widow for over a year now. Her husband had been one of the five thousand soldiers sent to Dieppe in the summer of 1942 and one of the ones that would not be coming home. She had come to the party only at the request of Tom, who thought that it was time for her to start having a social life again.

When everyone sat down to a table, John quickly slid in between Lily and Mrs. Johnstone, eager to have the seat beside Lily.

"I'm John," he said introducing himself. "Good of you to come with Tom tonight."

"He thought it would be a good idea to socialize with the people he will be working with for the next few months," she said, "and I am happy to spend time with him. I see him so little even though his base is so close to Toronto."

"Why is that?" asked John

"He's not allowed to leave the base," she replied. "He's only here as part of a mission. I know he leaves for Germany again in a few months."

"Why can't he leave the base?" John inquired. "This afternoon he said that people pretty much stayed there, but

I didn't get the idea that he was not allowed to leave. I just thought they stayed to be fair to the soldiers from far away."

"Do you know what they do at that base?" she asked.

"Not really. Isn't it just like any other army base?"

"No," she replied "The base trains commandos. They only take the best of the soldiers and train them to be commandos, snipers and demolition experts, with training to survive behind the enemy lines. Tom is the head of the training staff."

"Really?" John said surprised. "I knew that he seemed to be a good soldier, but I didn't know that he was that well trained. He made a joke about killing people with his bare hands earlier this week. I didn't think he had really done it."

"He may not have actually done it," she replied, "but he's more than capable of doing so. He could be the most mild mannered but dangerous person you'll ever meet."

"Good to know," John replied, suddenly thinking twice about wooing Tom's sister. His fears quickly disappeared as Lily smiled at him. "Care for a drink? Or something from the buffet?"

"Just a white wine, thank you."

John went to the bar and returned with two glasses of wine.

"Here you go," John said, sitting down again. "Cheers!" and they clinked glasses and had a sip.

"What is it that you do?" John asked

"Maternity ward nurse at the General Hospital. You?" asked Lily in return.

"I'm a mechanical engineering professor here, but for the past few months, I've been working with the team that Tom has joined."

"And your team is the reason he has to go back to Germany?" she asked.

"Unfortunately, yes," he replied, "although, with your description, I suddenly feel he might find this to be a boring assignment."

"Trust me," she replied, "if he's involved, there has to be something special about this assignment. They don't send him out of the camp unless it is something really important."

"I think our work is important," said John, "but perhaps the war committee has planned something that we don't know about. Maybe that's why Tom is here."

"Perhaps," Lily replied. "Anyway, I just hope he comes back safe again. I already lost my husband to Dieppe."

"I'm sorry," said John. "I didn't know."

"That's okay," Lily replied. "It's been over a year now. I'm used to him being gone. I just don't want to lose Tom too."

"Say, the band seems pretty good," John said, trying to change to a lighter topic. "Would you care to dance?"

"I'd be delighted," she replied.

Lily and John danced the rest of the evening. As midnight approached, they all gathered together for the countdown. "Five - four - three - two - one - Happy New Year!" the crowd yelled. Lily gave Tom a kiss on the cheek, then turned the other way and placed one on John's cheek.

John went home after the party feeling exceptionally happy, especially since he had asked Lily if he could take her out for dinner and she had said yes. "1944 is off to an amazing start," John thought to himself.

Chapter 13

Over the next three months, John and Lily had become a real couple. John took Lily out for New Year's Day dinner as had been arranged, and after that, they had dinner together almost every night. Most of the dinners were chaperoned by Tom, partially because he had to eat too, but also because he was the big, responsible brother. But Lily was an adult, a widow, and old enough to not need his input, and so John and Lily were rapidly falling in love.

The team had also been busy over those three months stockpiling a supply of FluorZi. As the end of March came around, the team approached and finally completed the twenty-five litres of FluorZi that had been ordered. They had outsourced the production of the pyramid containers and those were also completed and on hand by the end of March, including the twenty-five spare ones that had Ian requested to be used for training. Consequently, the first two weeks of April were spent inserting twenty-five millilitres of liquid gas into the pyramids for delivery to Germany. At the end of two weeks in April, they had completed the hundred units as requested by the order.

Ian called a meeting with George, John and Tom for Friday, the 14th of April. As usual, the meeting was held in the "meeting room" which was the name they had given to the rooftop café.

"As you are aware," Ian opened the meeting, "I've been sending regular reports to the war committee about our production levels. Today's report will inform them that the units are ready to be shipped to Halifax and onto Europe, but I do have a couple of issues that I would like to resolve before I send the report. First, how exactly are these to be shipped? At the moment, we have them just piled in the corner of the laboratory. I think they need to be packed into something for shipping."

"Actually," George responded, "I took care of that already. One of those request forms that you signed last week was for metal cases, like foot lockers. We can put twenty-five units into each box by putting rows of three pointing up and two pointing down between the three pointing up. As an extra precaution, we can fill the case with wax, that way the pyramids will be held in place during shipping. There is very little chance that one would break open due to jostling while in transit."

John interjected, "The other good thing about that method is that the loaded cases will sink. If it becomes necessary, the cases can just be dumped in the ocean. The pyramids would float by themselves, but in the metal box, they'll go straight to the bottom. And if the cases erode over time and the waxes start to leak, the gas will never make it to the surface; they'll react with ocean water and decompose."

"Ok, good," said Ian. "Can we have the cases packed and ready to go by next Tuesday?"

"I think so," replied George. "Wednesday at the latest."

"What about transportation to Halifax?" asked Ian.

"That's my responsibility," said Tom. "My orders are to arrange for a guard team from the camp to assist with transportation to Halifax. The camp has troop transport trucks and we can use a couple of them. I'll go to the camp on Monday and return on Tuesday with the trucks and the guards. We can set off for Halifax on Wednesday. We'll have to drive a little on the slow side so that we don't rattle the cargo too much, and that should get us there for Friday. Hopefully, the submarine will be there waiting."

"The cases should be able to withstand the bounces from highway driving," responded John.

"I didn't mean just the cases. The guards, anybody, in the back of the trucks, it's not the most comfortable ride."

"Okay, two down," said Ian. "Now for the most difficult issue. There was one part of the order that I did not read to everyone when it arrived at Christmas."

"And that is?" asked John.

Ian turned towards John. "The order 'requested', " Ian said using his fingers to make quotes when he said 'requested', "that at least one of our team accompany the pyramids to Europe. The order specifies we are to provide training to the European underground. I ordered twenty-five extra pyramid casings to be made just for that purpose. And since there's enough gas to kill everyone on the submarine a hundred times over, you're probably needed to ensure its safe transport."

Ian paused for a moment before continuing and also looked at George. "I think both of you should go with Tom. George, you're the chemist and responsible for the gas. John, you were responsible for the design of the containers. I think that if any field modifications need to be made once the pyramids are in Europe, both of you should be involved to make sure that any modifications are done safely."

"You're suggesting that we go to Germany?" said George, surprised.

"Unfortunately, yes," replied Ian.

"It won't be so bad," said Tom. "We're not going to try to cross any battlefields. We'll be going into the top of Germany. It's not guarded like the coast of France or the eastern front in Russia. There are some German troops there, but we'll be able to move around safe enough. And we're going to enter by boat at night, not by parachutes from a noisy plane."

"Well, when you put it like that," said John sarcastically, "who could say no."

"Relax," Tom said with a smile. "I've been behind the German lines on missions twice now. This one will be like a walk in the park, and part of my orders are to bring you back safely."

"Okay, okay," said George. "I'll go," he hesitated and then added, "but I'm staying close to you to make sure I get back safely."

"Okay," said John. "I guess I'm in too."

"There is no need to worry guys. I'll take good care of you. The only thing you need to worry about is the submarine ride."

"What? Why?" inquired George

"It's got to be over three thousand miles. Submarines only go about three to five miles per hour under water cruising and ten miles per hour at full speed. The trip is going to take at least four weeks on the submarine. They'll want to stay submerged a large part of the time. So, you've just signed up to take a trip where you'll be in a barrel that's a hundred yards long and ten yards wide. I haven't been on a submarine yet either, but I know the navy does a fair amount of training for submarine life. We're going without that particular training. The crew should be well trained though, so they will be able to help us adapt."

"Well," added John, "I think the way to think about it is that we'll be veterans of underwater life on the way back home."

"I'll notify the war committee that they should have the submarine ready for next Friday, and to expect three passengers, including Tom," said Ian.

"What do we bring?" asked George.

"Gas suits and any other equipment you think you might need, including equipment to test air samples. It would be good if you can squeeze it into a metal case like the ones for transporting the pyramids. The military will provide everything else, including clothing," said Tom.

With that, Ian adjourned the meeting, instructing Tom, John and George to enjoy their last weekend before the trip.

Chapter 14

That evening, George waited for Theresa to put Neville and Betty to bed. He made two coffees and took them to the living room and placed them on the coffee table by the fireplace.

"Theresa, come here and sit with me for a moment," he said. "We need to have a talk."

"Why do I think this is about something unpleasant," she said as she came and sat on the couch.

"You know we've been working on a project for the war effort. It was, and still is, top secret which is why I haven't told you much of what has gone on. The war committee in Ottawa has selected our project to be used in Germany by the underground forces."

"Excellent," said Theresa. "Did you just find out?"

"No, we've known since Christmas Eve," replied George. "We've been working to fulfill the order from the war committee. That's just the initial part of what I need to tell you. I just found out today that part of the war committee's request is that the underground forces receive training from us. Clearly, they cannot come to Toronto for training."

"So the training needs to happen in Europe," she interjected.

"Exactly. And as the lead chemist, Ian has suggested that I go to provide the training."

"Where? England?" Theresa asked.

"No. Germany. North Germany to be exact."

"You can't go to Germany. It's not safe there. You'd be behind enemy lines. You're not a soldier. They'll shoot you as a spy." Tears began to roll down Theresa's cheeks.

"Only if we were to get caught, but I don't think we will. I will be going with John and Tom. Tom is the commando captain that has been working with us. He's been to Germany for two missions already, and he says that this area is reasonably safe. We'll be a long way from the front lines, back where the German troops are mostly like police for the area. It's not an area that the Germans expect to be attacked so it is not well guarded, according to Tom. I've worked with him for a couple of months now in our lab. He is very capable and I think I can trust him to keep us safe."

"And who is John, the other person?"

"John is like me, another professor," said George.

"So, Tom has to watch out for two of you. I don't like it. I don't like it one bit."

George reached out and held Theresa's hand. "I know. It's not my choice either. But even though I'm not a soldier, it's my duty to help end the war in our favour. If that means I'm called upon to do more than just mix chemicals here, then I guess I have to go."

"How are you supposed to get there? And when? And for how long?"

"The army is providing trucks to take us to Halifax. We should be leaving on Tuesday. From Halifax, we'll travel by submarine to North Germany. That's why I think it's not too dangerous. We'll be underwater most of the time so we shouldn't have any troubles on the way. We'll meet up with the underground at night I guess, so we'll be a little hard to find. I've heard that the underground has gotten dozens of

70

escaped prisoners out of Germany, so they should be able to hide the three of us. I'm still not sure of all the details, but I think we'll be there by the first of June, and back sometime in July. Six to nine weeks, it seems."

"Tuesday...." sighed Theresa. "I'll make sandwiches for your drive."

"Hah," said George, "that's the spirit. I'll be home before you even know I'm gone."

Meanwhile, Tom and John had walked home to Lily's for dinner. Tom reassured John that this mission was much safer than the last two that he had done and he had survived those without a scratch. Both times, he had parachuted into Germany at night, and both times he had been helped out of Germany by the underground. He was confident that this mission would go off without a problem.

They were quiet all through dinner. Lily was suspicious that there was news, but she didn't try to pry it out of Tom. She already knew Tom was bound for Europe again. She guessed he was about to tell her that the time had come.

After dinner, the two helped Lily clean up, made her a pot of tea, and sat her down to tell her that both of them were going.

"I've been through this before," she said. "I know what to expect," Lily said with a croak, trying to stifle tears. "But God help you, if one of you comes back without the other I'll probably never speak to you again. Either of you."

Then she looked squarely at Tom. "You better bring him back unharmed. He's not like you. He's not prepared for this kind of work."

"Not to worry. That's why I'm going and not one of the less experienced recruits. You know I'll take good care of him."

"I know," she replied. Then she got up, took her tea to her room, closed the door, and cried.

George and Theresa spent the weekend playing with Neville and Betty and when the kids were in bed, they spent the time with each other by the living room fire.

Lily was up early on Saturday. She was scheduled to work the early shift at the hospital, and as always, she was on time.

When Lily got off work, John was waiting to pick her up with Tom's jeep.

"Tom loaned me the Jeep for the weekend," John said. "I was thinking that we could go to Niagara Falls for the rest of the weekend."

"What a wonderful idea!" Lily exclaimed.

"I can't take all the credit," said John. "Tom made the suggestion, and even contributed twenty dollars for the hotel and lent us the jeep."

"Well, since he is so encouraging, I guess we can't let him down," Lily laughed.

They went back to Lily's and she packed for the trip. She gave Tom a kiss on the cheek and left with John. The pair arrived at their destination in time to have a nice dinner and then checked into the hotel for the evening.

In the morning, they got up and went to view Niagara Falls. After watching the majesty of the falls for a while, they took a leisurely drive north long the Niagara Parkway to Queenston Heights where they enjoyed a lunch at the

Queenston Heights Restaurant. They had a window side table with a beautiful view of the Niagara River.

"Churchill did that same drive and ate here last summer," said John. "He described the Niagara Parkway as the 'the prettiest drive in the world'. Do you think he was right?"

"I don't know. He's been to many more places than I have. But it might be the prettiest drive I've ever done," replied Lily. "The view from here is magnificent too."

"Romantic?" asked John.

"Yes, when you're with the right person," said Lily with a smile.

"You know," John said, "we could find a Justice of the Peace tomorrow and get married before I go on this trip."

"No, John," Lily replied quietly. "Please don't be disappointed. I'll marry you the day you come back, but not the day before you leave."

"I'm not disappointed. Well, maybe just a little disappointed. I don't think you need to worry about Tom taking care of me anymore. Nothing can keep me from returning to you." He got up, went around the table, and gave Lily a huge kiss.

After lunch, they strolled, hand in hand, around the grounds of the restaurant admiring the beautiful view. Then they enjoyed a leisurely drive back to Toronto.

Chapter 15

As promised, Tom returned to Camp X on Monday and strolled into Darren's office.

"Tom, so good to see you," Darren said. "Surely your mission is not done yet."

"No, just phase one. I'm about to set off for North Germany, with two civilians no less. I just came back today to arrange for a guard troop to transport everything to Halifax."

"Not a problem. What do you need and when do you need it?"

"I'll need ten trainees, lightly armed. They all should be able to drive the transport trucks. And we'll head over to the university tomorrow to load up. Hopefully, we'll be on the road to Halifax by the end of the day, but definitely rolling by Wednesday. After we unload, they can drive the trucks back here. They can take turns driving."

"Fine. I'll have a squad and trucks ready to go tomorrow morning."

"I'm going to clean up some paperwork in my office, after all, there is a slight chance that I won't get back. Then I'll report to the barracks and get a good night's rest. I think it will be a long, but safe, trip."

While Tom was returning to Camp X, Captain Steve Hannan was on a training mission off the coast of North Carolina in the submarine USS Angelfish. When they surfaced, he received a radio broadcast order to put into port at the naval yard at Philadelphia and report to the office of Admiral Tim Wigless on Tuesday morning.

The USS Angelfish, launched in 1943, was a Balao Class submarine of the US Navy. The Balao class was the largest class of submarines used by the American Navy. Over three hundred feet long and twenty-seven feet wide, it housed a crew of eighty-two including ten officers. It was capable of top speeds of twenty-five miles per hour on the surface, ten miles per hour submerged and was certified to dive to a depth of four hundred feet. It was capable of being on patrol for seventy-five days without putting into port.

Captain Hannan was the USS Angelfish's first and only commander. His crew had been in basic training for several months and were very close to being ready to head to Pearl Harbour to participate in the battle of the Pacific. Steve was caught off-guard by the unexpected order to put into port. He was, however, duty-bound to follow orders and the Angelfish pulled into the Philadelphia Naval Yard on late Monday evening.

Eight o'clock on Tuesday morning, Captain Hannan was at the door of Admiral Wigless.

"Come in Steve. Please, sit," Tim said, gesturing to a guest chair.

Admiral Wigless sat on the edge of his desk. His informal posturing immediately put Steve at ease. Since he hadn't known the reason for the meeting, he had been a little apprehensive, but the relaxed attitude displayed by Tim eased Steve's tension. Now Steve was more curious than nervous.

"Your crew has been training for a while," stated Tim.

"Yes," agreed Steve. "We're almost ready to go to the Pearl Harbour."

Tim looked at his watch. "Well, about now, fresh supplies are being loaded onto the Angelfish. Your training is being ended a little early. We have a mission to be performed before you head off to Pearl."

"You've spiked my interest, Sir. Am I to understand that Pearl is not the destination?"

"Correct," replied Tim. "This should be an easy introduction to the war for your crew. Your mission is to ferry some cargo to North Germany. After the supplies are loaded, the Angelfish will head to Halifax where you will pick up three passengers and their cargo. You will take these passengers to North Germany to meet the European Underground near Cuxhaven. You will assist the passengers ashore and then remain in the North Sea until time to pick them back up. You will then return them to Halifax and report back here to me.

"My instructions are that it is imperative that this delivery go with as few problems as possible. As such, I want you to plot a route around the north side of Iceland and down along the coast of Norway. I realize that will add five or six hundred miles to the route, but I want the Angelfish out of the regular Atlantic traffic as much as possible."

"Understood Sir," responded Steve. "I think the only problem area on that route will be the North Sea. We could encounter German vessels in that area. After all, I understand that they have several ship construction sites along their north shore. We could run into a newly launched vessel or a patrol boat."

"Hopefully, you will not have to engage the enemy. However, we believe that you, your crew and the Angelfish are ready for anything that you may encounter."

"Do we know who the passengers are?" asked Steve

"Not exactly, but I have been informed that they are a commando captain and a pair of civilians. Their cargo is also secret, but all indications are that it is some kind of weapon for the European Underground to use and the civilians are responsible for training. That's why you have to stay around enemy waters until it's time for their return home. We can't have civilians cluttering up the war zone," Tim said with a small smile.

"Are all three coming back? Or is the commando staying in Germany?"

"As far as I know, all three are coming back."

"What about timing? How fast do we need to get there? And then how long do we wait?"

"Oh yes," laughed Tim, "I guess that would be good for you to know. They need to be there about the beginning of June. I'm not sure how long they need to stay ashore. Some of this will have to be determined when you meet the passengers."

"So," Steve paused, mentally performing calculations, "we're talking 3,500 to 4,000 miles. If we stay surfaced for the first part of the trip, we can easily do two hundred miles a day, then submerged for the stretch after Iceland and down into North Sea, about eighty to a hundred miles a day. We probably need about twenty-five to thirty days. We will have a little time to spare."

"You might need it. I suspect it might take a couple of days for the guests to get their sea legs. They probably have not been on a submarine, maybe not even been on a ship. Anyway, there will be an official order document in your quarters when you report back to the Angelfish. You'd better get underway as soon possible. The sooner you're on route, the more time you will have."

"On behalf of myself and my crew, thank you for the opportunity, Sir. I look forward to returning with a positive report of the mission." With that, Steve saluted and headed back to the Angelfish.

By the time Steve was aboard the Angelfish, the supplies had been loaded. The crew was curious as to what was happening. It was clear that something was in the works as they had been pulled from their training and the new supplies where waiting at the pier when they arrived. Steve went immediately to his quarters and reviewed the printed orders that were waiting in a sealed envelope. Admiral Wigless had summarized them well.

Steve called a quick meeting of the senior crew. He relayed the information to them about their mission, and they in turn, relayed the message to their subordinates, eventually disseminating the information to the entire crew. Within an hour of the meeting, the Angelfish was on its way out of the port and heading for the Halifax.

Chapter 16

Late Tuesday morning, two canvas covered transport trucks pulled up beside the U of T chemistry building. Tom jumped out of the lead truck, dressed in green army fatigues, complete with helmet and boots. From the two trucks came another ten soldiers dressed identically as Tom. The only difference was the rank markings on their arms. Eight of the soldiers waited at the trucks and two accompanied Tom into the building and down to the lab.

Daniel had been awaiting Tom's return to surprise him with a large rat that he had taken from the cages. From the doorway he saw that Tom and both of his followers were carrying holstered pistols in their belts. Daniel silently pulled back and put the rat back in the cage.

As they passed the door of the animal room, Tom winked at Daniel. "I saw that anyway. You'll have to try much harder to get a surprise over on me," Tom said with a smile.

In the lab, Ian and the rest of the team were packing the pyramids into the steel cases. John and George were filling one case with equipment. They stopped and came over to Ian and Tom.

"Ian, George, John, this is Sergeant Culeg and Sergeant Popolo," he said introducing the men. Everyone exchanged handshakes as Tom continued, "Sergeant Culeg will be in charge of Truck One, and Sergeant Popolo will handle Truck Two. Each of them have four helpers waiting by the trucks. We will have the men wait there until you've finished packing and then they'll load up everything. Can you show us what's to go?"

"Sure," said George. "There are six of the steel cases. Four have live pyramids, one has training pyramids, and one is the equipment John and I are bringing. Plus our duffle bags over there." He pointed at two duffle bags and a large basket near the door.

"You won't need those," replied Tom. "I have fatigues like these waiting for you. From this point on, you'll need to look like the rest of us. And, what's in the basket?"

"Sandwiches," said George with a smile. "Theresa made them so we won't be hungry on the drive."

"Those can absolutely come," said Tom, "but transfer them into two boxes, one for each truck. Leave the basket here."

"Are you through packing equipment?" asked Ian.

"Almost," John replied. "The equipment is all in. We just need the gas suits put in on top."

"Okay," said Ian. " The guys are just about done packing the pyramids. I'll have them pack the gas suits and split the sandwiches into a couple of boxes. Why don't you two go with Tom and his sergeants and get changed? Bring your clothes back here and put them in the duffle bags. After you're gone, I'll get them to put the duffle bags in your offices."

John and George went with Tom and the sergeants. Outside, Tom gave them the uniforms and they changed in the back of one of the trucks. While they were changing, Culeg and Popolo took the rest of the troops into the building and started bringing the cases out to the trucks. John and George went back into the lab in their new fatigues and stuffed their clothes into their duffle bags. Then they went back out and saw that Ian, Robert, Steve,

Shawn, Daniel, and the ten soldiers had put three steel cases and one box of sandwiches in each truck.

"Right then," said Tom, "it looks like we're ready to roll. John, you ride in the back of Truck Two with Sergeant Popolo. George and I will go with Sergeant Culeg."

A round of handshakes and "Take care" and "Good luck" followed as John, George and Tom said goodbye to the rest of their group. After the warm wishes, they climbed into the trucks, with three of the regular soldiers in the back of each truck, and two in front of each truck being the driver and navigator.

The men were bounced and tossed in the back of the trucks as they made their way through the city streets. Turning, decelerating, stopping, accelerating. After a few minutes, George said, "You weren't lying about this not being a comfortable ride. I don't think I can do this all the way to Halifax."

"Once we reach the highway it will not be so bad," replied Sergeant Culeg.

And true to his word, a half hour later, they were smoothly rolling east along the highway already outside of Toronto's city limits.

"Now that it's smooth," said George, "maybe we can have some of the sandwiches. I'm starving and it's past lunch."

"Great idea," said Tom. "Sergeant, open the sandwiches and tell us what choices there are."

Sergeant Culeg opened the box and looked up with a smile. "Just rabbit," he said.

"Theresa didn't make rabbit sandwiches," scoffed George. "I think they're all baloney."

"Maybe the other truck has baloney. All we have is live rabbit," Sergeant Culeg said as he tilted the box to show them the brown rabbit that was crouched inside.

"My fault," said Tom with a laugh. "I'm pretty sure I know who packed the sandwich boxes." He banged on the back of the truck cab and yelled, "Pull over to the side!"

The trucks pulled over, Truck Two following Truck One, and Sergeant Culeg got out. He let the rabbit go free on the side of the road and watched as it hopped towards the farmer's field along the highway. He went to the back of the other truck and split the sandwiches, with the help of Sergeant Popolo, from the very full box that was in the back of the second truck.

"Good thing you pulled over when you did," said Popolo. "We were about to have a feast!"

The trucks rumbled down the highway, stopping at Canadian Forces Base Valcartier, just north of Quebec City. After spending the night at the base, they crossed the St. Lawrence River at Quebec City and then continued east along the south side of the river. They turned south at Riviere-du-Loop and followed the highway through New Brunswick, past Fredericton and Moncton, and then crossed Nova Scotia to Halifax.

They had been driving below the speed limits to keep the ride as smooth as possible for the 'cargo', and occasionally they stopped for fuelling and food. It was just approaching the dinner hour when they pulled into Canadian Forces Base Halifax.

The camp had already been advised of their arrival and arrangements had been made for the unloading of the cargo and sleeping quarters for the crew. John, George and Tom were provided rooms in the Officer's quarters. Tom had provided them with army duffle bags containing extra sets of clothes and a spare pair of boots. They dropped their duffles in their rooms and met in the hall.

"We can eat in the Officer's mess," said Tom, leading the way.

Once settled in the Officer's mess at a table with their dinners, George and John were surprised at the quality of the food.

"It's very good," commented John. "I always thought that the food would be pretty bland and basic in the military."

"It varies," said Tom. "Between wars, the food does tend to get a little basic, but during war time, the government makes sure that there's good quality food provided to the troops, as best they can. It's easy to do that at Canadian bases, and harder to provide at the front lines, but they do try."

"Anyway," Tom continued, "now that we are just the three of us, I have something very important to discuss with you."

"Go on," said George in a hushed voice.

"Technically, you both are now commandos on a mission. Commandos don't use their real names in the field. As senior officer of our group, I have the honour of bestowing code names upon you. And it is an honour because these names will follow you for everything you do with the military from now on. Usually, we select names based on events from training, or some particular skill displayed in training. But in your case, I only have the few months of lab work from this assignment to go by."

John started laughing. "Oh, I can hardly wait to hear these names. I can just imagine the ones that have gone through your head."

Tom smiled, "If you were that darn Daniel, you would have cause to worry. But, I've picked a name for you that is more appropriate given your profession: Gears."

"Gears," repeated John. "I like that."

"And me?" asked George. "What have you come up with for me?"

"You were harder. I thought I'd pick something chemical, but most of the words are too long and complicated, like Erlenmeyer after the flasks that we used in the lab."

"Not fond of that," interjected George. "Erlenmeyer, who designed the flask, was German. Technically, the flasks we use are Buchner flasks because they are built with the vacuum hose attachment, but those are also German."

"Buchner is too long as well. It needs to be something that is quick and easy to say. One syllable is better in the field. In the end, I abandoned the chemistry theme. You are the doctor that designed the gas that started this whole adventure, so to make it easy, I decided to go with just Doc."

"Doc Beege," George said. "I can live with that. Doc and Gears. Yes, I think that works for us."

"What about you?" John asked. "What is your code name?"

"Bounce," Tom replied with a straight face.

George and John looked baffled. Where would such a name of come from?

"Puzzled?" asked Tom. "When we have successfully completed our mission, you'll have earned the right to hear the story behind my name. Anyway, from now on, no more use of Tom, John and George. No matter where we are, including here, try to use Bounce, Gears and Doc. That way, you'll get used to using those names as a reflex. Officially, however, for the purposes of this mission, you are Lieutenant Beege and Lieutenant Starchuk. Don't worry about learning the insignias for ranks. Once we're off this base, you outrank everyone except me and the submarine captain."

Chapter 17

First thing Thursday morning, Tom went to the base command centre and was notified that the USS Angelfish would arrive on Friday morning. He went back to the officers' barracks and woke George and John.

"What time is it?" said John groggily.

"Seven," replied Tom, "but you'll feel like it's six because of the Atlantic time zone. Come on, breakfast is waiting."

They ate in the officers' mess hall again. After a filling breakfast, they checked on Culeg and Popolo who were guarding the cargo. Since George and John had never been to Halifax, and the cargo was in good hands under the watchful eyes of the Camp-X men, Tom borrowed a jeep from the base's carpool and they spent the day touring Halifax, with a detour to Truro on the Bay of Fundy to watch the evening tide go out. Hours later, as the Bay of Fundy's morning tide was rolling in, Tom, George and John were fast asleep again in the officers' barracks.

At the same time in Hamburg, North Germany, Vorpostenboot 2110 Hermann Von Klink was sliding out of dry dock at one of the shipyards along the Elbe River, after having been equipped with a small cannon, depth charges and a new hydrophone. VP-2110 was a large fishing vessel before the war, one of the hundreds that the Kriegsmarine had repurposed as coastal patrol boats.

VP-2110 was commanded by Kapitanleutnant Horst Grunenburg. He was only twenty-nine years old and this was his first command. His crew was also inexperienced with respect to combat, although many had several years of experience as fishermen, being recruited into the

Kriegsmarine along with their vessels. As a young commander, his first assignment was not expected to be too demanding. After navigating down the Elbe and into the North Sea, they were to meet up with VP-2106 Ernst Schultz and spend the next sixty days patrolling north and south along the coast from Cuxhaven, Germany to Skagen, Denmark, and to Bergen, Norway.

VP-2106 was also a converted fishing vessel. VP-2106 sported the small canon and depth charges, but it had been converted before a hydrophone could be supplied for the vessel. VP-2106 was to patrol with VP-2110 for sixty days and then hand off the patrolling to VP-2110 and put into dry dock to be equipped with a hydrophone.

Kapitanleutnant Wilhelm Fischer was at the command of VP-2106. He was thirty-two years old and had been in command of VP-2106 for over a year, ever since VP-2106 had been converted from a fishing vessel. His heritage had been fishing, since Fischer meant fisherman, and his family had lived up to its name, having dozens of generations of fishermen over the past few centuries, including himself. He also had years of naval experience so it came as no surprise that he had been instructed to train Kapitanleutnant Grunenburg and the crew of VP-2110 so that they would be capable of patrolling the German-Denmark coast alone while VP-2106 was finally equipped with a hydrophone.

Earlier, Fischer had been introduced to Grunenburg, in port, by their commanding officer. The officer had suggested they go out for a meal and get to know each other since they would be working together. Once they were alone in the restaurant, Fischer spoke openly to Grunenburg.

"This training will seem very easy," he said. "We've been patrolling that coastline for over a year and have done nothing fruitful except harass small fishing boats and cargo transports."

"You have no actual combat experience?" inquired Grunenburg.

"Hah, no," Fischer replied. "Our experience is limited to occasionally firing a shell across the bow of a vessel that is slow to follow our orders. We've never even seen an enemy vessel. Look where they tell us to patrol. What enemy ship would come there? The water's cold, the towns are small. Most of that coast is uninhabitcd and has vcry rough terrain. If people wouldn't live there, why would the enemy even want to go there? There's nothing there for them, and it would be a stupid place to try to land an offensive."

Fischer sighed and continued, "No, we're doomed to a boring patrol. The best that either of us can hope for is that we get promoted to a larger vessel by typing our boring reports perfectly."

"Maybe you're patrolling too close to the coast. They won't come that far east."

"No, we don't patrol the shallows," Fischer replied. "We zig-zag a route that is twenty to eighty miles off of the coast. We don't see the enemy because the Royal Navy spends more time in the Atlantic and English Channel than the North Sea."

"Maybe the enemy has submarines operating along the coast?" suggested Grunenburg.

"Maybe, but without a hydrophone, we could have easily passed over many submarines without ever knowing," Fischer replied. He shook his head. "But, I don't think so. If we had crossed a submarine, I'm sure they would have let us know they were there by blowing us out of the water!"

Fischer waved his arms to emulate an explosion, which then had both of them laughing.

"We'll have a hydrophone when we launch," said Grunenburg seriously. "I plan to get the operators well practiced while we patrol with your crew. If a submarine should come, it will have to deal with the both of us."

Chapter 18

Mid-Friday morning, a radio signal was received at CFB Halifax indicating that the USS Angelfish was waiting about two miles off the shore.

Tom had his soldiers load the steel cases onto a camp barge at the dock. There was a round of handshakes, and many "Farewells", "Good lucks" between Tom, George, John and the soldiers. The three men boarded the barge and headed out into the Atlantic to meet the submarine.

"A good sign," said Tom, looking around. "The ocean is fairly calm today. That will make the cargo transfer easier and our first day's ride smoother."

Back on shore, Culeg, Popolo and the soldiers headed for the trucks.

"How much money do you have?" Culeg asked Popolo.

"I don't know. Why?"

"Captain Wallace's orders were to drive back to the camp. He didn't say how fast. After all, it is Friday. I was thinking if we all pool our money, we could spend the weekend in Montreal and be back on base on Sunday night in time for lights out."

The men gathered in a group and discussed Culeg's suggestion. Collectively, the ten of them had $205 and some change, enough to get through a fun weekend in Montreal.

George, John and Tom stood at the bow rail of the barge and gazed out towards the horizon. Nothing but waves were visible for as far as the eye could see. Suddenly, the bow tip of the submarine blasted through the surface like a breaching whale. As more of the vessel came up, the bow came smashing down to the surface as the vessel levelled off. While still over a quarter of a mile away, the three were impressed with the sight of such a large vessel almost instantly appearing from nowhere.

The submarine was almost exactly as Tom had described. It looked like a pointed tube that was as long as a football field, with a small hut in the middle. The submarine quickly slowed to an idle speed as the barge bounced in the waves produced by the surfacing vessel.

The barge slowed along the side of the submarine and ropes were lashed to it. Almost immediately, several sailors appeared on the submarine's deck, popping up out of hatches. One appeared at the top of the small hut and climbed down the ladder that was affixed to the side of it. The sailors all quickly snapped to attention as the man approached the barge. He extended a hand and helped Tom, with his duffle over his shoulder, up onto the deck.

"Welcome aboard," he said as he and Tom helped John and George, along with their duffle bags, up onto the submarine. "I'm Captain Steve Hannan, and my vessel is at your disposal."

"Pleased to meet you," said Tom. "I'm Captain Tom Wallace and these are Lieutenants Beege and Starchuk."

Steve gave Tom a peculiar, puzzled look, tilting an eyebrow, but after a moment, he turned to the crew on the deck and ordered them to bring the gear from the barge and stow it below. Within an instant, two of the sailors were in the barge and had begun passing the steel cases up to the others.

"Hey, easy with those," said George. "They're delicate."

"What are they?" asked Steve.

George started to answer but Tom cut him off. "Just the equipment we are taking with us to Germany. Some of the components and gauges are glass and a little fragile. We've packed them well, but no point in shaking them any more than necessary."

Steve turned towards the crew and ordered, "Gently stow those cases below."

He turned back to the three men. "We've arranged quarters for you as well. Unfortunately, we are a little cramped for space, so your two Lieutenants will have to share a suite," he said with a bit of a grin. "Follow me."

John and George looked at each other. "A suite?" they whispered to each other in unison.

They followed their host down through a hatch on the deck of the submarine. Once inside, they were amazed at what they were seeing. John, the engineer, was especially appreciative of the work that had been done to fit so much into such a small space. The forward hatch, where they had entered, placed them onto the upper deck inside the submarine in the forward torpedo room. They could see the torpedoes strapped to dollies locked onto tracks, ready to be placed in the tubes. Towards the rear, it looked like a long hallway.

"Two floors?" asked Tom.

"Yes," replied Steve as they started walking towards the back. "The hatch we came in put us in the forward torpedo room. The lower deck is mostly storage holds and batteries. The upper deck has officers' quarters in the front half, including a meeting room, then the control room, then the galley, crew quarters, engine rooms and finally the aft torpedo room."

They were walking as Steve spoke. Every time they passed a sailor, they had to turn sideways as the corridor was very narrow. Steve stopped in front of a room. "This will be your room Captain Wallace. Just drop your duffle inside. You can unpack shortly."

John and George noticed that Tom's room seemed to be only about thirty square feet, with a bed on the wall, a locker and a small sink.

"Suite?" whispered George to John as they continued down the hall.

"This is the control room," Steve said as they entered an area that was packed with dials and gauges. Men were jammed in along either side and each seemed to have just two or three feet of work space.

"Ahead full. Stay surfaced," Steve instructed the man that seemed to be in charge of the area. They felt the machine engage the engines and begin to move forward. To their surprise, it was a very smooth motion.

Steve continued, "This is the galley." John and George started miming eating to each other as they understood that the galley was the kitchen and dining area.

"And now we are entering the crew quarters. This one will be your quarters, Lieutenants." They had stopped in front of a pair of lockers, one of several on either side of the hall. "Place your duffles inside and we'll go back and sit in my meeting room."

That's when it dawned on them why the Captain had smiled when he said 'suite'. Their 'suite' was two of three beds mounted on the wall, one below the other, and lockers for their clothes to be hung. The room had twelve sets of beds, each set being six beds, three high on each side.

"How many people are on this thing?" asked George.

"We are running with nine officers, and seventy crew. Actually with you three aboard, we are at capacity as there are only ten officers quarters plus bunks for seventy-two crew."

John and George dropped their duffles into the lockers.

"Do they lock?" asked John.

"Why would they?" responded Steve. "It's not like anyone could take something and get away."

"No, I suppose not," replied John. "I guess that's one of the nuances of submarine life."

"One of several, as you will find out soon enough," laughed Steve.

They proceeded back the way they had come to the meeting room in the officers' quarters.

"I'm sure you noticed that there are bulkhead doors between each section. That's so we can seal a section in the event of a breach," Steve explained as they entered the meeting room.

"Please sit," Steve said. The room was small, with a round table and five chairs. No room for any other furniture. "Perhaps you can clear something up for me. We seemed to have deviated from the information I was provided. I was under the impression that two of you were civilians."

"Yes," responded Tom, "they are actually civilians. However, my commanders felt they would blend in better if they appeared to be soldiers, so we've made them Honorary Lieutenants for the mission. Besides, if something goes awry in Germany, as Lieutenants, they will be treated like POWs instead of shot as spies."

"That's a relief," John said uneasily.

Ignoring the comment, Tom asked Steve, "What else do you know?"

"Only that I'm to get you to Cuxhaven by June and then wait for you to complete your mission and return you all back to Halifax."

"Good," said Tom. "For now, that's all you need to know. How likely are we to get there by June?"

"Oh, very likely, I should think. We'll stay surfaced and put in about two hundred miles per day until we round Iceland, after that, we'll only get about eighty to a hundred miles per day. We're much slower submerged, but of course, far less visible.

"We could go a little faster in the beginning, but I want to be below surface for a few hours each day so that you three get accustomed to being underwater. You can feel the difference in the pressure and it takes some getting used to. After Iceland, we'll try to keep underwater most of the time, just surfacing to recycle air supplies and check in with the Coastal Command by radio."

"Where is our equipment?" asked George.

"The lower deck has some storage rooms below the control center. Your equipment has been secured there," Steve replied.

"Well then," Steve continued, "now that we're underway, and you've seen the living conditions here, I don't know what you can do to keep yourselves occupied for the next four weeks, unless you'd like to volunteer for crew positions."

"I think so," said Tom and George and John nodded in approval.

"Doc here," Tom continued pointing to George, "he knows some chemistry. Always mixing things up. Perhaps he could help out in the galley? And Gears is good with mechanics. Maybe he could help with the engine room?"

"Good," said Steve. "And you?"

"I'm the soldier here. Weapons are my area of expertise. Point me towards the torpedoes."

"Sure," agreed Steve. "Okay, why don't you go and unpack your duffles. I'll notify the chef, the engineering officers and the weapons officers to include you three in the duty rosters. And now I'm going to take us under for a few hours, so you can start getting used to being underwater."

They headed back to their lockers to unpack. Steve followed John and George but stopped in the control room.

"Take us down to a hundred feet," they heard him say as they entered the galley.

Chapter 19

Tom, John and George quickly adapted to life on the submarine. The crew was very helpful and patient with the newcomers and didn't seem to mind taking the extra time needed to demonstrate or explain the way things were done on the submarine.

The three were also glad to be working with the crew, but for different reasons. Tom and George quickly realized that it was difficult to fill free time on the submarine; there was just not much to do. That was much less true for John, who was like a kid in a candy store. He marvelled at the engineering that had gone into designing and building the submarine, and he was using his free time to investigate the various mechanical systems from end to end on the ship. Tom and George were just content to work with their assigned departments.

After fourteen days they were still on the schedule that Captain Hannan had described. They had travelled about 2,700 miles and had passed around the top of Iceland. Admiral Wigless' desire that they stay out of the normal Atlantic traffic had also come true. They had not seen another vessel, friendly or foe, civilian or naval, since they had passed north of Newfoundland. But now, they had curled south and were heading through the North Sea towards Cuxhaven. The next 1,300 miles would go much slower as they were staying submerged most of the time and only running on the surface for several hours in the middle of every night.

John noticed that the diesel engines were not running when they were submerged, and he studied the propulsion system. Tom and George were very surprised when John described how the system worked.

"The diesel engines are actually just big generators. There are over two hundred tons of batteries on the lower deck, the biggest batteries you'll ever see. I'm surprised this thing doesn't go straight to the bottom with all that weight. As the diesel engines run they charge the batteries. The batteries can last for about forty-eight hours. Electric motors are then used underwater to turn the propellers. The electric motors are much quieter than the engines, so when underwater, the hydrophones have a harder time hearing us."

"What's a hydrophone?" asked George.

"It's a microphone system for listening for noises in the water. Sounds travel well in water. So, if they were to use the diesel engines below surface, they would be easy to hear because of the noise. You wouldn't be able to stay hidden underwater. The electric engines are much harder to hear. It would be hard for a ship to detect a submarine with the hydrophone if other ships were nearby."

"Doesn't our side use hydrophones too?" asked Tom

"Yes and no," replied John, enjoying lecturing to his friends on the things he had learned around the ship. "Our surface ships are equipped with SONAR, which uses echo location sound technology like a bat. It sends a noise and then listens for the echo. The changes between the original sound and the echo can be used to calculate both direction and distance. Submarines, on the other hand, don't use SONAR because the sound can be heard on hydrophones, so SONAR would give away the position of the submarine. Our submarines have hydrophones, but ours are just forward facing because there is too much interference from the submarine itself to listen in other directions. I don't think they would work well at detecting something approaching from behind."

The next ten days went by just like the two previous weeks, except now the submarine was moving much slower, cruising underwater at about three miles per hour for eighteen hours a day, and then eight miles per hour for the six hours in the middle of the night. Since they were angling south from Iceland towards Norway, the submarine only surfaced at night as it was far more difficult to be seen by other ships then.

Just after midnight on the morning of May 15th, VP-2110 and VP-2106 had reached the northern end of their patrol. They negotiated a 180 degree turn to the south and they were cruising at about fifteen miles per hour back towards Germany.

Late on that same morning, Tom found Captain Hannan on the bridge. The Captain looked like he was concentrating as he was looking through the periscope.

"Sorry to interrupt," Tom began. "I'm just curious, Captain. Where are we exactly?"

Steve lowered the periscope. "We're about fifteen miles off the coast of Norway, a 150 miles south of Bergen."

"What's Bergen?"

"That's the largest city along the coast of Norway, about half way from top to bottom. You can see the coast because the coast is mountainous. Would you like to have a look?"

"Sure," said Tom eagerly.

Steve raised the periscope and turned it to look to the east. "There. Have a look. You can just see the mountains on the horizon."

"Oh yeah," said Tom, looking through the periscope. "This is neat."

Tom began turning the periscope to see forward, then west, then north behind them. All three directions seemed to be nothing but ocean waves and blue sky, but as he started to turn to look east again, something caught his eye.

"What's that to the north?" asked Tom.

"Let me see," said Steve, pushing Tom out of the way. Steve stared through the periscope, sweeping left and right, searching the horizon behind the submarine. Suddenly, he found what Tom had seen. Far on the horizon, two patrol boats were gaining on them. He lowered the periscope.

"Turn starboard thirty degrees and take us down to two hundred feet. Now!"

"Enemy ship?" asked Tom.

"Yes. Two patrol ships," said Steve. "Let's hope they didn't see us."

Chapter 20

Kapitanleutnant Grunenburg, aboard VP-2110, woke early on May 15th and after a light breakfast, reported to the bridge. "Anything?" he asked the hydrophone operator. He had made it his habit to check with the operators every hour that he was on duty.

"Just VP-2106," came the operator's reply.

"As usual," smiled Grunenburg. "Don't you ever get tired of hearing them?" he said referring to his patrol partner.

"We are all so familiar with their engine noise, it has become part of the system. In fact, I'm not sure what it will be like when they are in dry dock. We might miss their noise," the operator responded with a laugh.

Grunenburg laughed too. "Keep up the good work," he said. He was pleased with the development of the operators. Even with the constant noise from VP-2106, they had honed the ability to pick out sounds from other engines that were several miles away. He was a little disappointed that the sounds they had found so far were just small fishing boats and transport freighters. He had joined the Kriegsmarine to fight, not to harass old sailors.

The two patrol boats continued their standard zig-zag pattern for a few hours. Late in the morning, the hydrophone operator frantically signalled to Grunenburg. "Kapitanleutnant, Kapitanleutnant," he repeated several times. Grunenburg came over to him. "I'm hearing a new sound," he said. "It's very faint, but I can hear it. It's straight south of us."

"Another fishing boat?" asked Grunenburg.

"No Sir. It is a different sound than any of the other boats we have identified before. It's a constant whirr sound, not like the pulsing noise that engines make. I think it might be a submarine."

Grunenburg went directly to his wireless radio operator. "Send a question to Kriegsmarine Command. Ask if there are any of our submarines operating in this area. Then get on the shortwave and send a message to VP-2106 that we believe we have found a submarine due south and are altering our course to intercept."

Grunenburg turned to the helmsman, "Ahead full, south!"

When Fischer received the message from his radio operator, he also ordered his helmsman to go to full speed and follow VP-2110. He grabbed his binoculars and began to scan the horizon ahead of them.

"Bring me a radio so that I can talk to Kapitanleutnant Grunenburg directly," Fischer ordered his radio operator.

As Fischer's operator retrieved a handheld radio for him, Kriegsmarine Command sent back a message to VP-2110 that there were no known submarines in their area.

VP-2110's operator brought the message to Grunenburg along with a handheld radio. "Kapitanleutnant Fischer wants to talk to you directly," he said, handing the radio to Grunenburg.

Before responding to Fischer, he turned to his operator. "Update?"

"Still south," came the reply.

"Fischer, Grunenburg here. Our hydrophone has caught a submarine due south, we believe. And it's not one of ours."

"Good," replied Fischer. "Our first enemy vessel. You'll have to track it and we'll parallel your manoeuvres. I'm looking for it too."

"Radio back if you see anything," Grunenburg replied. Then he turned to the operator and instructed, "Tell us the status every five minutes, and anytime that the direction changes."

For the next half hour, the operator called "Still south!" every five minutes and twice he added, "And it's louder. We are closing the distance."

Grunenburg relayed the updates to Fischer as they came. Both of them were excitedly scanning the seas ahead with binoculars.

Finally, Fischer radioed, "I'm positive I saw a periscope, but it went under already. It was straight ahead. Maybe they saw us too. Listen to see if they turn."

"Ahhh," said Grunenburg. "The game of cat and mouse has begun."

Grunenburg turned to the hydrophone operator. "Fischer saw the periscope. It went under. Direct us."

"They turned to starboard, Sir. If we go twenty degrees to starboard, we should be above them in about three minutes."

"Twenty degrees starboard," Grunenburg ordered the helmsman and VP-2110 turned.

VP-2106, following the other ship's movements, turned as well and positioned themselves about two hundred yards parallel and half a boat length behind.

"Mimic their direction changes," Fischer ordered his helmsman.

On the Angelfish, Steve did not wait to find out if they had been seen. "Cut the engines, then turn us to the north. Let our momentum carry us."

The crew immediately executed the manoeuvre.

Back on the VP-2110, the hydrophone operator yelled, "I've lost the sound!"

"They're gliding. Trying to hide. We're almost overtop of them," Grunenburg yelled into the radio to Fischer. "Depth charges on my mark ..... NOW!"

With that order, VP-2110 dropped two depth charges off their stern. VP-2106 also released two. A few seconds later, a fountain of water exploded from the sea surface, followed by another and then two more in the wake of VP-2106.

Below the surface, the Angelfish was rocked by the four explosions, but did not sustain any damage. The ships had overshot the position of the Angelfish, partially because of the glided turn, but also because the ships were moving much faster than the submarine.

Steve was knocked to the floor as the compression waves shook the Angelfish. "Ahead full!" Steve called and the helmsman engaged the engines and shifted to full speed. Full speed underwater was still much slower than the ships, but at least they were moving in opposite directions.

"I hear them. They're behind us," called VP-2110's hydrophone operator. The ships slowed and turned to chase.

Neither the patrol boats or the submarine were exceptionally manoeuvrable, but it would take time for the ships to slow to execute large turns. Time that Captain Hannan planned to use. For the next hour, Steve played hide and seek with the two ships. The Angelfish accelerated, turned, glided, turned, dived, accelerated, rose, varying directions, depths and lengths of time.

Occasionally, the submarine pointed towards the ships, after the ships had passed overhead or after a series of turns, and their position was reported to Hannan by the submarine's hydrophone operator. The ships reacted to the submarine's movements when they could hear with the hydrophone, taking advantage of their faster speed to close back in every time the mouse had curled away. Each time they believed they were close, they dropped more depth charges. And each time, the Angelfish was shaken but not significantly damaged.

Chapter 21

Tom, John, and George were on the bunks in the crew quarters, alone. All the rest of the crew had trained for defending attacks and had places to be within the submarine. John, Tom and George thought it best to stay out of everyone's way.

"Why don't we shoot back?" asked George.

"We can't," replied John. "We need to be closer to the surface."

"And use the periscope to aim," said Tom. "It's too dangerous."

"More dangerous than waiting for one of those charges to be close enough to destroy us? I wish we could blow something near them and give them a taste of their own medicine," complained George.

"Doc, you're a genius! What temperature is it outside?" said Tom enthusiastically. John's eyes opened wide as he realized what Tom was thinking.

"Yes! It's midday. It has to be easily into the seventies," said John. "We can't give them a taste of their own medicine, but we can give them a whiff of our medicine. A deadly whiff."

"Of course, but how? We need to get them to the surface," asked George, excited as he contemplated the plan that was forming.

"Bounce, go to the bridge. Tell Hannan that we have a bomb that we can send out of the torpedo tubes. Tell him it can destroy both of the attacking ships but we need to have them get close," said John. "Doc, go below to the hold and get two pyramids and meet me at the aft torpedo room. I'll get the other things we need."

The three leapt from the bunks and began to run to their separate destinations.

"Bounce," George called after Tom, "we need to know the depth!"

"Hannan, Hannan!" called Tom as he entered the control room.

"Not now," replied Steve, who was huddled with the other senior staff, discussing the next avoidance manoeuvre. They had a map spread out on the table and were plotting their course changes and their best guesses of where they thought the ships would be.

"Yes now! Doc and Gears have a bomb we can send to the surface to destroy those ships," Tom continued.

"Who and what?" exclaimed Steve.

"John and George," replied Tom. "Their cargo cases contain bombs. John thinks we can expel them through the torpedo tubes and surprise the ships. We just need to bring the ships in close."

"We'll only get one chance if we do that. Will they work?"

"I haven't seen one used, but from what I know of how they work, I'm one hundred percent positive they will. Those two geniuses believe it will and I trust them completely."

Just then, the Angelfish shuddered again and again as two more depth charges exploded.

"They're getting closer," said Steve with a scowl on his face. "Ahead full, turn ninety degrees to port." Then he turned to

Tom, "Let me know when they're ready and I'll lure them in close."

"How deep will we be?" asked Tom.

"Fifty feet," replied Steve.

While Tom was informing Captain Hannan of the plan, John had gone to the aft torpedo room, grabbed a notepad and pencil and began jotting down calculations. The crew in the torpedo room looked at him like he was a crazy lunatic.

"Get me a drill. And a three-eighths or quarter inch bit. And some wire, and some large wrenches and some wood," John ordered.

The crew looked bewildered. "Where would we find wood on a submarine?" one asked.

"I don't know! Cabinet doors in the Captain's quarters? Think! Look Around! Now sailors!" he yelled and they jumped into action.

"You," he said to the one nearest the torpedo tubes, "get a tube ready to expel a surprise for the ships."

"Yes Sir," the sailor said enthusiastically with a smile.

John returned to his calculations. Moments later, the Angelfish shuddered from the two recent depth charge explosions.

Within the next two minutes, the sailors had returned with an electric drill and the other requested supplies, followed by Tom and at last, George. George was bleeding lightly from his forehead because he had fallen on the stairs during the last shake from the depth charges. One sailor had two cupboard doors that he had appropriated from the galley. "The captain's cupboards are nicer, but I'm not going to get them," the sailor said.

"Your design is rugged, Gears," George said. "I dropped both of the pyramids when I fell and we're still alive."

"Great," said John. "Drill holes into the four bottom corners of each pyramid so we can attach these wires. Then use the drill to make a hole in the cupboard doors large enough for the tip of the pyramid to stick through, about two inches."

Tom held the pyramids steady as George drilled four holes in each.

John was checking the weights of the wrenches. "Too heavy, too heavy, good, heavy, good," he said as he tested the various wrenches with his hand. He pushed the two good wrenches towards Tom.

"What are we doing?" Tom asked.

"We need to put a weight on the bottom, otherwise the pyramids might float upside down. The wood at the top and the weight at the bottom will keep them upright," replied John. "String the wire diagonally in a cross at the bottom so the wrench is suspended about six inches below the centre, then use the wire to attach them to the wood."

Tom began affixing the wires, wrenches and wood to the pyramids. When he finished, he held one of the boards out flat. The wires suspended the pyramid below the board with two inches of the pyramid poking through. The wrench, acting as a counter balance weight, dangled below the middle of the pyramid.

"Perfect. The wood will be like ground level. It will be as if they're buried in water," said George, pressing on his cut to stop the bleeding.

"Once we put these in the torpedo tube and close the door, how long until they can be launched?" asked John.

"We need about thirty seconds to build up the air pressure in the tube to launch the items and open the outer doors. Why?" replied one of the sailors.

"We need to know how long to make the fuse," replied George. "How deep will we be?"

"Hannan said fifty feet," replied Tom.

"Good," said John. "I'll set the fuse for about ninety seconds. That should give it enough time to get to the surface."

Tom ran back to the control room. "We're ready. We need about ninety seconds for us to light the fuse, put it into the tube and get it to the surface."

"Fine," said Steve. "I'll bring us to periscope depth and put up the scope. That will give them something to look at. Then we'll dive to fifty feet. I'll try to guess when they're about two minutes away before we dive. That should get us to fifty feet and I'll tell you to launch. The timing is all guesswork. I hope we are close enough when the bomb goes off."

"From what I know, we don't need to be too close. The bomb has a hell of a range," assured Tom.

"Stay full ahead, turn another ninety to port and bring us to periscope depth," Steve ordered the control room crew.

Chapter 22

The patrol boats had just turned again after having dropped the latest depth charges. They were both originally large fishing boats, and at higher speeds, the turns took several minutes to execute. The Angelfish was exploiting this weakness and used those moments to turn as well and accelerate away.

Grunenburg had noticed this exploitation; the submarine would wait for them to start turning and then turn in the opposite direction. He guessed that the submarine had a forward hydrophone.

"Can you hear them? Where are they?" Grunenburg yelled at the hydrophone operator.

"They turned to their port, but now it appears they've turned again. They're running away from us, but straight ahead."

"Excellent. Stay sharp," Grunenburg said. Then he picked up the radio. "They're running away again, straight ahead," he called to Fischer.

"Great," Fischer responded through the radio. "Let's try to get on either side of them and drop our depth charges together. One of them will hit even if they turn."

"Agreed," replied Grunenburg.

Grunenburg and Fischer continued to scan forward with their binoculars. About thirty seconds later, a periscope broke through the surface.

"Periscope ahead!" Grunenburg yelled into the radio.

"I see it. Maybe they are surfacing to surrender. Hold the course so we can come along both sides," Fischer replied.

"Agreed. We'll get medals when we return with our capture," Grunenburg replied.

"Wait," came Fischer through the radio, "they're diving again."

"Those fools," Grunenburg said smugly. "They've given their position away and we're too close for them to escape. We'll be over them momentarily. This time, we'll blow them right out of the water."

A few moments later, debris from the submarine broke through the surface.

"Debris ahead," Fischer said into the radio. "Stay on the quarry, we'll slow and check the debris. It might be a trick."

VP-2110 raced forward to get above the submarine. They were now heading south by south-west. VP-2106 slowed to collect the debris, but nothing came over the side to collect the debris. The ship glided past at the same speed, but on a slightly more eastward angle than VP-2110. No one even looked over the rails of the ship at the two boards floating at the surface.

"Cut the engines, turn forty-five degrees starboard, glide to a hundred feet deep," Steve ordered the submarine control room crew. "Keep performing evasive manoeuvres. I'm not gambling that we're in the clear yet."

But after two minutes, there were no more depth charge explosions. Steve waited five more minutes and still nothing happened.

"I can hear them south by south-west of us," the Angelfish's hydrophone operator informed Steve. "And they're a ways off too. They passed over without dropping depth charges."

"Bring us to periscope depth," Steve ordered.

Steve raised the periscope on the bridge and scanned around for the ships. He found them on the horizon, and travelling away from their position.

An hour later, Kriegsmarine Command radioed to VP-2110 and VP-2106 to get an update on the submarine. The German ships were now fifteen miles south by south-west from the area where the submarine had been encountered. The message was received by the ships, but no answer was returned.

Chapter 23

Steve asked for Tom, George and John to join him in the meeting room. When they were all seated, Steve started the meeting.

"We spent over an hour trying to hide from those ships. Then we launched your bomb. But it didn't destroy the ships as you said should happen. I saw them with the periscope heading south by south-west. I don't know why they stopped their attack, but they definitely weren't destroyed."

"There's more than one way to destroy a ship," Tom replied. "Tell us, what is south by south-west of us?"

"Depending on the exact degree, there's a row of islands across the top of Germany and Holland. A little more west of that would be the top of the English Channel."

"Well," said George, "there will be a lot of damage to those two ships when they ram into one of those islands. But if they miss those, and wander into the English Channel, I'm sure they'll be sunk by an Allied destroyer."

"I'm sure they will change course before either of those events," said Steve.

"That would require someone alive on board to change their course. We're quite sure that those ships will stay on their current course until they run out of fuel, or hit something. We expect that both crews are dead," replied George.

"How?"

"Our bombs don't explode in the way you were thinking. They released a toxic gas. Both those ships went through a gas cloud and everyone on board would have died almost instantly. Fast enough that they wouldn't have been able to send out a distress call for help."

"If you're correct, the Kriegsmarine will be wondering where they went and why they're not responding to radio calls," said Steve.

"Perhaps," said Tom, "but we could get lucky and they could be sunk by air attacks or maybe they'll run across an Allied ship that will send them to the bottom."

"When we surface tonight I'll radio for air patrols to watch out for these ships. Maybe we can make some of our own luck that way," Steve grinned. The smile then slid off his face when he realized that his submarine was carrying more of these gas bombs. "How many of these gas bombs are still on board?"

"Ninety-eight," said George.

"So you brought an even hundred and used two to attack the ships?"

"Yes," said John. "One could have done the job, but I wanted to double the chances of success. We may have wasted one."

"Now that I know what's in those cases, I'll be glad when they're off the ship. We're still about ten days away from putting you ashore."

"Actually, Captain, we are ahead of schedule for landing. Our orders were to arrive for the beginning of June. With your permission, I'd like to take the opportunity to circle back to the point of the detonation," George paused, "...what is it that you military folks call that point?"

"Ground zero," replied Tom.

"Ah, yes," George continued, "I'd like to go back to ground zero and take air samples to see how long before the gas cloud dissipates and the area is safe. Our research showed that water was a good buffer, but we never had the opportunity to test effectiveness over open water. I'm not surprised at all that it worked against the ships, but I'd like some readings on how far it ranges and how long it is effective."

"What do you need? And remember, we can only surface at night. In the day, we're too easy to spot from the air," Steve reminded the group. "I'll take your word that you were able to neutralize a ship, but an air attack might be safe from even a moderate height."

"Can we proceed today in a straight line until we can surface? That will put us about twenty-five or thirty miles from ground zero," George requested.

Steve mulled it over for a moment. "Alright. We can stay under for twelve hours and then it will be in the middle of the night when we surface."

"Perfect. I can take an air sample there and then tomorrow night, can I take an air sample at ground zero?" asked George.

"I guess we can do that. Just hope they don't get another patrol boat in the area," replied Steve.

"If another ship comes through before the gas is neutralized, they will not be a threat to us," Tom said with a laugh, but then he froze with the realization that the air above the submarine could still be toxic. "If you go out to take an air sample, and it is still dangerous, how do you get in and out without contaminating the air in the submarine when you open the hatch door to come back in?"

"That's Gear's job for the next ten hours. Gears, you have to figure out a way that I can go out and come back in without endangering the rest of the crew. Either neutralize the gas in the air I bring in with water or extremely high heat," George said with a grin.

Chapter 24

When the meeting ended, John immediately went to find the Angelfish's lead engineer. He and his crew were just finishing some minor repairs caused by the shaking the vessel had experienced with the depth charges. Their last repair was two makeshift cupboard doors in the galley.

John and the engineer spent a few hours in the meeting room. The meeting table was covered with the blueprints of the submarine and the diagrams of its various systems. In short order, those documents were covered with diagrams and sheets of calculations done by the two of them. Eventually, they agreed upon a plan that they believed would work.

George spent time in the galley, preparing dinner for the crew. With the attack over, the crew had returned to normal activities and dinner needed to be served on schedule. After dinner, George helped with the dish washing then he went to his bunk and tried to sleep. Knowing that he could be awake through a large portion of the night, he was determined to be as well rested as possible.

George had managed to only get a few hours of sleep when John came and woke him.

"Doc, we need to practice the procedure in case the air is still contaminated," John said.

"Did you figure out a way that is safe for me to go out and back in? How can we do it?"

"One thing about submarines, they have very sophisticated systems for moving water. Did you know they actually pump in water to dive, and then pump it out to surface?"

"No. I thought it was the fins on the side that controlled going up and down."

"They're part of the control, but the real way it works is by controlling the density of the vessel by adding or subtracting water to the ballast tanks."

"Okay, but how does that help me?"

John looked at George with a sly grin. "We're going to help you the same way Mother Nature helped Margaret."

"I'm going to need more details than that."

"The engineers are almost finished rigging a set of pipes to the roof of the forward torpedo room. They've essentially doubled the existing sprinkler system to spray water. We're going to close the bulkhead to the torpedo room and use the pumping systems to force water through those pipes and create a hell of a rain storm inside the room. Then we'll pump the water back out. Fortunately, almost everything on the submarine is designed to survive getting wet. We will be relying on you to determine when it will be safe to open the bulkhead. Unfortunately, you're going to get a little wet. Well, the gas suit should keep you dry, but it will get wet. Come on, let's go practice."

They went to the forward torpedo room. As described, the engineers had rigged up a set of pipes that looked like a building fire sprinkler system. John and George reviewed the operation with the engineers and they worked out a set of tapped signal patterns that George could use to signal to outside the torpedo room by banging on the door with a wrench.

John and George stayed in the torpedo room and the engineers left, sealing the bulkhead behind them. A moment later, George tapped the code to start the pump and suddenly they were standing in the middle of a torrential downpour inside the submarine. In less than a minute, both men were thoroughly soaked.

"Do you think this is good enough?" John shouted.

The sprinklers were too loud and George couldn't make out the words had John said. "What?" George yelled back.

"Do - You - Think - This - Is - Good - Enough?" John yelled at the top of his lungs.

"Almost," George yelled as he picked up the wrench and tapped the code to turn off the water. Next he tapped the code to turn on the draining pump. A few moments later, the water was drained from the room and they opened the bulkhead. John gave the thumbs up signal to the engineers who responded with a whoop and a cheer.

"Very good work, but I'd like to request two modifications," George said. "First, can there be a hose attached to the system? The gas is heavier than air, but it would still be good to be able to spray water all the way up to the escape hatch door. And second, can the hot water tank be connected to feed water to the system? It's almost summer but that water was damn cold."

John started laughing, even though he was shivering too. "Okay. Go dry off and we'll see what we can do."

A half hour later, John, still dripping wet, came to the crew quarters and found George. "Doc, you need to go do one more test."

"Fine," George replied and started heading toward the bow of the ship. John didn't follow.

"Are you coming, Gears?" George said back over his shoulder.

"No Doc, one wetting was enough for me. You get to test your modifications on your own," John said with a grin.

George did just that. Shut in the torpedo room, he tapped the code to signal to the crew to start the rain and he tested the spray of the hose up towards the escape hatch. The hot water had been mixed in so the resulting spray was warmer than before. George thought that it would be quite tolerable, enough that he figured he could stay in the room until the water was almost waist deep. He thought that would be more than sufficient to neutralize all the gas and not damage the gas suits. He tapped the codes to signal to switch off the water and start the drainage pump.

Chapter 25

Tom and Steve were waiting outside the torpedo room when the bulkhead door was opened. As it was Steve's ship, he wanted to have some idea of how John and George planned to take and test the air samples and keep the crew safe. Tom was also worried for George - what if George was killed trying to get the samples? Their worries melted away for a few precious seconds when the door opened and they saw George standing in the door way, dripping wet. Tom and Steve were overcome with laughter. When they stopped, George explained the method of neutralizing the gas that John had created, explaining that the gas compound was quite reactive when it came in contact with water.

"One thing has been bothering me," Tom interjected. "One thing we did not consider when we made our plans before. If the air is still contaminated where we surface, we won't be able to recycle the air of the submarine. If we return to ground zero to test tomorrow night, we will be very close to the forty-eight hours that we can be running on the ship systems."

"Not true," said Steve. "The forty-eight hours is a restriction for the battery charges only when we're running at full speed, submerged. The air system on the submarine can actually last for several days without problem. We are not a full day from ground zero so we won't run full tilt to get back so that will use less battery power. The diesel engines also have their own dedicated air and exhaust paths through the hull to the outside so we can run the engines as long as the contaminated air won't damage them, re-charging the batteries."

"So, we can safely go to ground zero and if the air is still contaminated, we can go a full day from there and test again?" George asked.

"Yes," replied Steve with a nod. "What I'm trying to say is that if that last test is contaminated, we can go a full day further away from ground zero and hopefully that air will be fine. If it's not, we may then have to cause to worry."

"We're south of ground zero now, right?" George asked.

"A little to the west of south."

"Then if the air is contaminated at ground zero, I suggest we go west as air typically moves towards the east. West should find clean air sooner," suggested George.

"We're only about twenty miles from ground zero now. And ground zero was only about twenty to thirty miles west of the south tip of the Norwegian coast. If the air is contaminated over that much of a range, then we may have to alert the Norwegians," said Steve with a frown. He didn't want to do any of this, the doubling back for testing, carrying the gas bombs on his submarine. He knew, though, that it was necessary for the war effort to have these scientist have their best understanding of how these weapons worked.

Steve's frown deepened as George said, "If the air is bad here, it may be too late to warn them. We didn't consider all the after effects of releasing two gas units."

Steve took a deep breath. The damage would already be done. Then, a thought occurred to him that he voiced to George and Tom. "Air movement would typically be more of an east by south-east direction. That would push it from ground zero into the straight between Norway and

Denmark. We may have caught a piece of luck there." He prayed they had.

"Now that we're considering this," said George, "let's decide on where to take a second sample depending on the results tonight." Tom and Steve nodded and George continued, "Now, let me go get changed. You guys are dry, but I'm still soaked to the bone."

George dried off and then spent the next hour in the submarine's store room, preparing the equipment to do the air quality test. At about one o'clock in the morning, the submarine surfaced. George put on his gas suit, took his equipment case and was sealed alone in the torpedo room. He set up his equipment and then climbed up the ladder to the escape hatch. George took a moment to steady his nerves, then opened the hatch a little ways, bringing the night air in. Even though the sea was calm and the skies were clear, George didn't go up onto the deck. If he slipped and fell off, no one could come help him. He stayed on the ladder and collected his air samples through the open hatch door. He took a moment to admire the stars, the moon, and their reflections on the calm sea before closing and sealing the hatch and carefully climbing back down the ladder.

Once back inside the room, he proceeded to test his air samples for the presence of FluorZi. He quickly found that the air still contained just enough FluorZi to be lethal. Next he took a sample of the air in the torpedo room and tested it. It too also contained a lethal level of the gas, just from the hatch being opened for a short period of time. George quickly put his equipment back into his equipment case, closed it and set it on top of a table to protect it from the impending rain storm and the water that would be collected in the room. Then he picked up the wrench and tapped the code to signal the crew to start the storm. Just as before, the water came blasting from the sprinklers and George used the hose to spray up to the escape hatch door. Unlike his regular clothes, the gas suit was fortunately more protective, the water just bounced off and he stayed dry inside.

Once he believed that it had run long enough, he tapped the code to stop the water and start the draining. While it was draining, he quickly set up his equipment again and tested the air quality of the room. Clear and safe. He tapped the code to let the others know that the air inside the torpedo room was clear. He had given Tom and John strict instructions that if they didn't hear the 'all clear' code, and he did not emerge as planned, no one was to open the bulkhead door.

As the last bit of water drained from the room, he removed the head piece of the suit and opened the bulkhead door. Seeing George alive and well, without the head piece on, was an immediate relief to Tom, Steve and John and the rest of the crew anxiously waiting outside the torpedo room door.

Chapter 26

"Status?" asked Steve as George stepped through the door.

"The outside air is lethal, relatively weak, but still dangerous," replied George.

"Okay, we won't recycle air tonight," Steve responded. "Get changed and join us in the meeting room."

George got out of the gas suit and stored the equipment back into the storage hold on the lower deck. He went up to the meeting room where Tom, John and Steve were waiting.

"Now that you're out of your gear and dry, can you give us a more detailed summary of your tests?" asked Steve.

George nodded. "I opened the escape hatch and took an air sample from there without going up onto the deck. Then I sealed the escape hatch again. The hatch was only open for about two minutes. Then I tested the sample to determine the concentration of FluorZi, and I found a weak, but lethal concentration of the gas in the sample.

"Next, I sampled and tested the air in the torpedo room. It too had a weak but lethal concentration, so the gas came in fast enough when the hatch was open to create a lethal concentration in the room. The concentration in the room was a little weaker than the outside air, but still lethal. Then we ran the water system to neutralize the room. I re-sampled and tested the air in the torpedo room and found the rain system had effectively neutralized the FluorZi."

"Great work, John, George," said Tom. "Given the concentration you found, how long do you think it will take to naturally neutralize?"

"Another day and it should be clear," replied George. "How far are we from ground zero?"

"About twenty-five miles I would guess," responded Steve. "I can get a more accurate distance from the navigator if you need that for your notes."

"No, the estimate will suffice," said George, looking contemplative.

"S'matter?" asked John

"Nothing," replied George, "just thinking." But he wasn't just thinking. He was rapidly performing calculations in his head, and keeping the calculations to himself.

"Well then, where would the best location be for the next test?" asked Steve.

"I think we should go to the east of ground zero since that would be nearest the shore. It should be clear by tomorrow night, but I'll sleep better knowing the coast is safe. It may have been a better idea to have gone there first. We should also do a test at ground zero, just to be complete in our research," said George.

"I believe we're far enough ahead of schedule to be able to do the two tests," added Tom.

"We should still have twelve days to go about three hundred miles," said Steve. "I think we should do your two tests and then cruise towards Cuxhaven in a zig-zag pattern. I don't want to get too close to the north shore of Germany until May 30th at the earliest. If we arrive too early, it's likely that there will be no one there to greet you. Better to arrive on the scheduled date."

"Also," Steve continued, "while we were surfaced, we radioed a message for air patrols to keep an eye out for those two German patrol boats."

The next day passed quickly. The submarine moved east to a point south of the bottom tip of Norway and George ran an air sample test. They followed the same procedure as earlier, with the internal rain system still in place, but George was able to stay dry as the air quality test indicated it was all clear. Nevertheless, George did a second test just to be sure.

While they were surfaced doing the test, they received notice that a Bristol Beaufighter aircraft of Coastal Command had torpedoed and sunk a German Patrol boat in the area that the Angelfish had reported. The patrol boat had not provided any resistance during the attack.

During the next day, the submarine returned to ground zero and George repeated the tests once again. The tests showed that the air at ground zero was now clean.

During this second test, they received another radio communication that another Bristol Beaufighter aircraft of Coastal Command had torpedoed and sunk a second German Patrol boat still in the area that the Angelfish had reported, again with no resistance.

After that, it was business as usual as the submarine slowly made its way south towards Cuxhaven, zig-zagging as Steve had suggested.

Chapter 27

Marino and Saco were brothers. They were born and lived all their lives in Kolobrzeg, Poland, a small village on the North coast of Poland, not far from the border with Germany. Living on the southern edge of the village, their youth had been spent playing and hunting in the forests and fishing in the Parseta river with their best friends, William and David. For as long as anyone could remember, no one ever saw one of them without the other three.

Marino was the oldest, two years older than his brother. Tall and well built, he was the ringleader of the four. Even though he was the most physically dominant of the group, his role as leader was not due to his size. He was the leader because he was the planner. Marino was not lazy, but he always had a scheme brewing in his brain to get ahead via the easiest route. Those around the village who knew him considered him to be a mild trouble maker and were always wary of his offers. If he offered to remove some garbage, there was a high probability that he thought he could sell some or all of it for a profit.

Saco was the "numbers" guy. Being the younger brother, he was not a natural leader and he tended to follow along on his brother's adventures. But he was a quick thinker and could quickly analyze the profit potential of his brother's plans. Even though the villagers were aware that Marino always had an ulterior motive, most were not aware of the number of plans that Marino made and Saco stopped because the profit would not be as high or as easy as Marino had initially believed. Together they made a good pair. Creativity balanced by rationality.

David was the same age as Saco. They had been classmates in school since the beginning of their school years. It was only natural that David and Saco became close friends because, apart from school mates, they were also neighbours. David's family lived on the same block as Saco and Marino. David, however, was not the quickest thinker. Usually he didn't do anything without being directed by Marino or Saco. His speciality was that he was good with his hands. He had an affinity for mechanical things and could fix almost anything. He was also creative in the sense that he could design and build things. He wouldn't be the one to have the initial idea, but if Saco or Marino asked for a tool to do some specific action, David would find a way to build it. Consequently, he was an excellent addition to the group. Creativity, Rationality, Repair.

William was, by age, in between Marino and Saco. His family also lived near Marino and Saco, just one street over. William had hunted and fished with the others because of proximity, but he had not been their classmate. William's family was Jewish. Because he was friends with Jews and non-Jews, he knew a larger group of people than Marino, Saco and David, and that broad set of contacts was the skill he brought to the group. William was the one who could get things. If the group needed something, William would reach out to his numerous sources and could get it. Creativity, Rationality, Repair and Supply. Everyone brought a special something to the group.

Marino was only twenty years old when the Germans invaded Poland in 1939. William was nineteen and Saco and David were both eighteen. They had been hunting in the woods when the German troops came into Kolobrzeg and took control. Their familiarity with the terrain allowed them to stay in the woods undetected and they saw their families, friends and classmates rounded up and taken away from the village. They hid in caves and thickets in the woods and avoided capture by the regular patrols. It didn't take long however, before the prey became the predators and the patrols started suffering casualties from ambushes by the group of four or from traps and snares designed by David.

The group had survived the last four years in the woods by continuing to hunt and fish, stealing supplies like guns and ammo from the troops patrolling in and around the village, and getting some supplies from the villagers that had been left by the Germans. The Germans had only taken the Jews and the families that they believed could be put to work in factories supplying the German forces. The undesirables had been left in the village to survive on their own and it was difficult for the remaining villagers to survive when the most productive inhabitants were carted away. Still, the villagers that were left helped the group whenever they could.

The group's reputation as nuisances to the German troops in the area spread and before long, they came into contact with others that were also resisting the Nazi invasion. Through these contacts, the Polish government, who were in exile in England, had become aware of this group and the foursome eventually became part of the Polish Home Army. The Polish Home Army was the largest underground resistance organization in Europe. Their branch of the organization was headquartered in Gdansk, approximately 120 miles to the east of Kolobrzeg.

Near the end of May, they were summoned to a large meeting in Gdansk. The meeting was held in the basement of a theatre during a music performance. The underground members were able to attend by mingling with the patrons of the theatre, having been provided special tickets to get through the front door. If someone had stood outside the theatre and counted, they would have realized that there were about seventy-five more patrons than seats in the theatre, but even the German officials in attendance at the performance didn't notice the patrons that went down the stairs to the basement, especially since most of the Germans were directed up to the prestigious balcony seats. Those going up the balcony access stairs didn't pay close attention to those going down the other sets of stairs to the basement.

The meeting was led by Peter Donalski. Peter was older and heavyset, with grey hair. Peter's family ran a metal works factory in Gdansk that had made metal plumbing components before the war, but the factory had been transformed to produce artillery shell casings for the German army. Working on contracts for the military had helped Peter establish a level of trust with the Germans governing the area. Having that level of trust meant the Germans did not monitor all the activities of the factory, making it an excellent headquarters for the local underground operations, which Peter covertly directed.

The meeting agenda had only two items. The first was the news that the Allies were planning a large offensive sometime in June. There was no information about where or how it was to happen, only that it could be expected. The message from England stated that the underground would need to immediately step up their raids as the additional activities of the underground across Europe would help distract the Germans and assist in keeping the actual location of the invasion from being discovered.

The second item was a request for volunteers to pick up three Canadian commandos who would need assistance with their mission in North Germany. The Canadians would be coming by submarine and would need to be met off the coast of Cuxhaven, Germany. Marino, knowing William could get a boat and David could make it run, volunteered the group for the mission. Since the group was known as a team that could successfully hide in the woods and remain undetected if necessary, the attendees confirmed them as the team to go.

To make the four hundred mile trip to Cuxhaven, Peter would be providing the foursome with a cube truck and papers to show that they were factory workers being sent to pick up new machinery to bring back to the factory in Gdansk. The back of the truck, however, was fitted with a false wall that could be used to hide cargo and even a few people if necessary. The inside length of the storage was about six feet shorter than the outside length.

On May 31st, the group got word that the submarine would be off the coast of Cuxhaven that night. The group began preparing to make the lengthy trip from Gdansk to Cuxhaven. The truck was fuelled and ready, and they were provided with purchase telegrams for machinery to be picked up in Cuxhaven on June 1st. The four men noticed that the papers were real. The company in Cuxhaven was owned by a family that had Polish heritage and remained undetected in the city. With the invasion of Poland, the family had remained loyal to their heritage, and without the border, had actually found it easier to communicate with relatives in Poland through business communications. Coincidentally, the main relative that they communicated with in Poland was their cousin, Peter Donalski.

The young men took turns driving during the long trip. Three could fit in the front, but they split into pairs with two riding in the front while the other two sat in the back of the empty truck. Twice they were stopped by German patrols to have their papers checked and both times they were asked why there were four of them on the trip. Both times they had replied that it was a long drive, the equipment was heavy, and four people were needed to share the driving and lift the machinery. Both times the German patrols accepted the answers and sent them on their way. Little did the Germans know that both times, Saco had calmly dealt with the patrols while a seething Marino sat quietly, hiding the pistol he held tight against his leg.

When they arrived in Cuxhaven, they went straight to the factory and loaded the equipment. The owner had arranged for the group to stay at the home of an employee that he trusted. After loading the truck, they went to the employee's home and were treated to dinner. Afterwards, William and David wanted to go down to the harbour to see if there was a boat they could steal later that evening. To blend into the neighbourhood, the employee sent his wife with them. Two strangers wandering around would draw attention, but being escorted by a local person, they would likely go completely unnoticed. Their mission was a success as they found a small barge that they could easily get out of the harbour undetected with the cover of darkness.

While William and David were gone, the employee drew a map for Marino and Saco to show them a wooded area along the shore where they could beach the boat and unload the cargo. It would take a few minutes to load the cargo into the truck as they would have to unload some of the equipment to open the false wall of the truck. But the patrols inside of Germany were fewer than in Poland, and the group surmised that the woods would provide the cover they needed.

Chapter 28

Tom sat in his quarters on the submarine, turning the sealed envelope over and over in his hand. Earlier, Steve had told them that they would be able to rendezvous that night with members of the underground that would help with the next stage of their mission. With a deep breath, he carefully tore open the end of the envelope and removed the message contained inside.

Dear Soldier,

You have been selected for this mission by Major General Darren Reed, a commander that we trust implicitly, and so we trust you implicitly to carry out these orders without fail. You may be our last hope.

As you are aware, the weapon you are delivering to Europe has devastating potential. What you may not be aware of is that the quantity you possess, if used simultaneously, has the potential to obliterate a major portion, if not all, of Germany. Unfortunately, depending on the winds and weather, portions of the countries sharing borders with Germany may also he impacted.

There will be an invasion in the early part of June. If the invasion is successful, we will have the foothold in Europe we need to sweep across the continent. If the invasion is successful, you are to return to Canada without delivering the weapon. But if the invasion fails, it is almost a certainty that the war will be lost. Under this grave circumstance, you are to take the weapon to as close to Hanover as you can and deploy all of it simultaneously. Future generations may judge this action as a war crime, but we fear the alternative

*future of the world should Germany be victorious. The
end will justify the means.*

*Our direction is that you rendezvous with the
underground and wait for news of the invasion. Do
not allow them to become aware of the kind of
weapon you are carrying or its devastating potential.
After that, we will relay a message to the
underground to proceed or abort. If your target is
identified as Hanover, you are to proceed with
deployment. If the target is identified as Cuxhaven,
you are to abort and return to the submarine
immediately.*

The letter was signed, as his friend and commander Darren
had predicted, by the highest name that Tom could
imagine.

Tom blew out a long breath, folded the letter back into the
envelope and tucked it away inside his jacket pocket again.
He now understood the importance of this mission. The
Allies would be throwing everything available at the coming
invasion. If it failed, there would be little left to stop
Germany from invading England and eventually North
America. In that event, the only chance for victory would be
the complete annihilation of Germany.

Deep in the back of his mind, he wanted to discuss the
orders with Doc and Gears, but the soldier in him told him
to keep these directions confidential for as long as possible.
At some point, he may have to inform them, but for now,
Tom decided that they just needed to be instructed that the
existence of the weapon and its power could not be shared
with anyone until they received instructions after the
invasion. He also decided not to tell them that if the

invasion was successful, the pyramids were to leave with them.

Tom asked to meet with Steve, Doc and Gears in Steve's meeting room.

"I don't know if you are aware, but I am carrying orders that I was instructed to read upon our arrival in Europe. I have read them now and I can bring you up to date on some things at this time. Some parts are still confidential and I will inform you of those parts when the time is right," said Tom with a serious expression.

"Why can't you tell us now?" asked George.

"Welcome to the army," Tom replied with a small grin. "If something happens to me, you are to continue with the orders that you have been given. That's just how things work with the army."

"So, you're saying our orders will change?" inferred John.

"His orders may change. That may or may not affect your orders. That's all you need to know for now," interjected Steve in support of Tom.

"Here's what you can know," continued Tom. "There will be an invasion of Europe soon. I don't know where or exactly when, but it will be shortly. I'm very sure that it is not at Cuxhaven. Our mission would be impossible if we were caught in the middle of the attack. We are to rendezvous with the underground tonight, but they are not to know what we are bringing until after the invasion. We will be instructed when to tell them about the weapons and when to start their training. That means we are to remain with the underground until after the invasion and Steve will have to stay in the area and wait to pick us up. They know how much longer Steve can keep the submarine out without re-supply, so I'm sure they've timed our trip to be near the invasion date. For all I know, it could be tomorrow."

"I think we will be able to stay in the area for another two weeks without much trouble," said Steve. "Just remember that it might take us a full day to get back to the rendezvous point."

"And nothing has changed much for us," added George. "We're still being picked up by the underground. The only thing new is that we know there will be an invasion soon and that we must keep the pyramids a secret until after the invasion."

"So, tonight we get off the submarine and go with the underground? Do we bring the pyramids?" asked John.

"Yes," replied Tom. "We need to be in position to execute immediately after the invasion."

"And," added Steve with a grin, "I'm much happier with that cargo staying with the experts that know how to handle it."

George looked at John. "Remember last November, we thought the Air Force would be too afraid of FluorZi? I guess we can add the Navy to that list," he chuckled.

"I suggest that you three get some sleep," said Steve. "You only have a few hours before we'll be at the rendezvous point."

Tom, John and George went back to their bunks and tried to sleep. It was a little easier for Tom, as he had the private bunk. John and George had a harder time sleeping because the crew quarters were essentially a hallway and the submarine was active twenty-four hours a day. They were both also feeling quite nervous about the potential danger that lay ahead when they left the submarine and entered enemy territory.

The crew woke the guys at two o'clock in the morning. They had already brought the cases up to the forward torpedo room. George, Tom and John found Steve on the bridge looking through the periscope, scanning the shoreline and watching for the signal which was a short flash of light followed by a long flash and then another short flash. At about three o'clock, as agreed, he saw the flashes.

"Our friends have arrived. Bring us to the surface and full stop," ordered Steve.

Ten minutes later, they were on the surface and standing on the outer deck of the coning tower. Steve was watching through binoculars for the signal again. The protocol was to flash the signal every fifteen minutes. Flashing too frequently could attract attention, but intermittently, they would likely go unnoticed. After a few minutes, they all saw the signal, even without binoculars.

"Make two short flashes in that direction," Steve said to Tom, pointing towards a spot on the shore.

Tom used his flashlight to make two quick flashes in the direction that Steve indicated. The flashes were answered with one quick flash.

"They've seen our position," Steve said. "They will be here shortly. It will take them a couple of minutes to get out here from the shore."

Saco and William arrived at the submarine quicker than Steve had expected. To speed things up, they had been waiting in the barge already off of the shore. They pulled the barge alongside the boat and the submarine crew lashed the barge to the side of the submarine.

"Three Crows?" asked Saco.

"Flying east," replied Tom, completing the coded greeting.

There was no further talking as the submarine crew loaded the steel cases onto the barge. Tom, George and John all saluted Steve and then climbed aboard the barge. Steve watched the barge disappear into the darkness of night and then followed the crew below. A moment later, the submarine dove and was out of sight.

Chapter 29

It was a quiet boat ride to shore as no one tried to speak over the noise of the barge. William brought the boat into the shallows and gently beached it in the area that had been identified by the factory employee. Marino and David were waiting on the shore. They had already unloaded some of the machinery they had picked up from the factory so that the steel cases and the three commandos could hide behind the false wall.

"I am Saco," Saco said once everyone was off the barge. "This Marino, William and David."

"Bounce, Doc, Gears," replied Tom pointing at himself and then the other two.

"You must excuse," said Saco "My English not good. They English not good too. You speak Polish?"

John opened his mouth to answer but Tom saw him and immediately cut him off before the Polish men noticed.

"No. None of us speak Polish," Tom confirmed.

"Is okay," said Marino. "We talk English. Load boxes now."

The group quickly moved the cases from the barge to the hidden storage of the truck, as directed by Saco. Once the truck was loaded, David went over to the trees and began to relieve himself.

"Do like him," William said. "Long time in truck."

The three quickly clued into the message. They followed suit as did their other hosts.

When everyone was ready to leave, David and William got into the front of the truck and the others got into the back.

"We go five hours," Saco said. It had become apparent that he would be the spokesman for the group as his English was the best of the four.

"If German patrol, they bang wall of truck," said Saco, pointing over his shoulder to the front of the truck. "You go there with boxes, we push machines in way. Let you out after pass patrol."

As Saco had predicted, the trip was just over five hours before they reached their destination. Just as the Polish men were stopped twice on the way from Gdansk to Cuxhaven, they were also stopped twice on the way back. Both times the three Canadians quickly slid behind the false wall, and the machinery was pushed against it to complete the disguise before the truck had come to a stop. The first patrol took a quick look at the machinery and decided that it was too much work to inspect the truck in detail and sent them on their way. The second patrol that stopped them had been one of the patrols of German troops that had stopped the Polish men on the way in. Remembering them from the previous day, they sent the truck along with just a quick look through the back door.

It was now late morning and they all got out of the truck. The Canadians noted that the truck had been parked in a barn.

"Where are we?" asked Tom.

"Near Kolobrzeg, our home," said Saco. "This farm is friends. Eat here, then Gdansk."

They followed the four up to the farmhouse. The old farmer and his wife had food waiting for them. They crowded around the table and had a lunch of cheese, bread and fresh milk.

"This is your home?" asked George.

"Friends," said Saco. "We lived in Kolobrzeg before war. Now we live in woods."

"We, how you say, Robbing Hoods," added Marino. "Live woods, rob Germans."

"But give to us," added Saco, causing everyone to laugh.

Chapter 30

After lunch, Tom, John and George went out onto the porch. They stretched to get rid of the stiffness that had developed during the morning ride.

As they were still waiting for their local hosts to come out, John whispered to Tom, "You know my family is Polish? I speak Polish fluently. Why did you cut me off before?"

John whispered back, "I don't want them to know. They will probably say things to each other thinking we don't understand. Maybe something important that they weren't planning to tell us. They may be on our side of the war, but let's not give away any advantages we may have."

"Right," agreed John. "I'm too trusting, I guess. I'll have to remember to be more careful."

"For the next few days, don't trust anyone except Doc and me. No one is on our team."

Moments later, their hosts came out, saying good-bye to their farmer friends. Everyone got back in the truck and made the uneventful trip to Gdansk.

The truck backed into the loading dock at the factory in Gdansk where Peter was waiting for them. After introductions, Peter led them through the factory. The factory was in operation, but the employees, being Polish, did not pay attention to the frequent visitors that Peter brought through the plant.

Peter's command of English was very good. He had gone to school in London so he spoke English with an accent that was a combination of the British and Polish accents, which sounded strange to the Canadians.

Peter explained what the factory was producing as they walked through the plant. Peter then led everyone to the upper level of the factory offices. This area had been transformed into living quarters, and was a large open room with eight sets of bunk beds, a small kitchen in the corner and a table with six chairs. Peter explained that the room was used often by members of the underground when staying in Gdansk. There was also a private bathroom at the far end of the room.

Peter informed them that they could stay in the factory offices for as long as necessary. He warned the Canadians that because they did not speak Polish, they shouldn't be on the streets in case they were stopped by the German authorities. The Canadian group agreed to stay in the office's living quarters and Peter suggested that Marino's group stay with them, as security.

The office residence was safe, but dull. There was little to do but watch pedestrians on the streets of Gdansk from the safety of the office windows. Peter had not been misleading them about the German authorities. They regularly watched German troops stop and check the identification of pedestrians at random. John estimated that a stranger would likely be stopped the first or second time they were on the street. Fortunately, four stories above the street was sufficient to allow for them to watch without being noticed by the people below. Other than watching the streets, the seven men told stories of their youths to each other to pass time. The only disruption was when the office ladies brought meals up to the room. Even though there was a kitchen in the room, Peter had meals prepared and sent up to them.

On the morning of June 4th, 1944, Peter came up to the office residence.

"There is a rumour," Peter said in Polish to Marino's team. *"Odilo Globocnik will be coming to Gdansk this afternoon to meet with the local SS. If this is true, we need to take advantage of the visit and assassinate him."*

"We can do this," replied Marino, also in Polish. *"We can stop him on the way into Gdansk. Do you know the time of the meeting?"*

"It's supposed to be at three o'clock."

Marino nodded. *"Good, then we have time to get into position about two hours ahead of the meeting."*

Peter, Marino and his team discussed for a few moments about the location of the attack and the equipment they would need. They had a pile of maps on the table and were examining a map of the Gdansk region. Tom had not understood any of what was said but he had recognized the name Odilo Globocnik. He went and sat beside John and whispered, "What's going on?"

"They're planning a raid," replied John in a whisper. "Can we help?"

Tom shook his head and whispered, "No, it is not part of our agenda. We have our orders. They're on their own."

After Peter and Marino's team had left, Tom asked, "Do you know exactly what they are planning?"

"Yes," replied John. "They are going to try to stop the car of a German official as he comes into town. He should be in a typical staff car. They should be able to spot it as it comes along the highway. They've got machine guns and will spray a hail of bullets to stop the car as it passes."

"Amateurs..." Tom said, shaking his head. "They should have asked for advice. Their plan relies on luck to be successful. I hope they succeed, but don't be surprised if they come back having failed."

George went to the pile of maps on the table and found a map of Germany. He spread it on the table and was moving his finger around the map. He appeared to be counting.

"What are you looking at?" asked John.

"Just looking at the locations of major cities. There aren't really that many. Lots of small cities, but not many large cities like Berlin or Munich. How big do you think Germany is?"

"I don't know ...." John trailed off, thinking. "About a 100,000 to 150,000 square miles, I would guess."

"Yes, that's what I would guess too," said George. "It's smaller than a lot of provinces in Canada."

"That's not really a surprise," said Tom. "From Quebec to BC, all those provinces are bigger than many countries."

"I just think it's interesting," said George. "It just gives me some perspective on the scale of things."

John and Tom exchanged puzzled glances, but did not say anything further.

The three men went back to their usual routine, had lunch, and waited for the others to return. In the late afternoon, Peter came up to wait with them. He looked very nervous.

"Problems?" asked George.

"The men went to do a raid. They should have come back by now. This plan is not good in any way. Globocnik is a monster. He needs to be eliminated. But he has status in the SS. If they fail, he will continue to be a monster, maybe worse because he was targeted for assassination. But if they succeed, the SS will tear Gdansk apart looking for the perpetrators."

"The timing is in your favour. If they succeed, hopefully the invasion will provide enough of a distraction that they are too occupied to worry about one assassination," said John in an attempt to comfort him.

Shortly after, Marino, Saco and William returned, clearly upset.

"*Where's David?*" asked Peter in Polish.

"*They shot him. He's dead,*" replied Saco, trying to hold back the tears.

"*How did you get away? Are they coming for you?*" asked Peter, concerned that they would all be discovered.

"*No,*" said Marino. "*They are not coming. They don't even know they shot him.*"

Tom, watching the exchange between Peter and Marino, and the upset faces of the group asked, "What happened?"

"*We were waiting, lying behind the trees along the road. David was in a tree, watching for the car. He was to signal us so we could rush out and spray it with bullets,*" Marino said in Polish, with Peter translating for George, John and Tom. "*But, they came down the road with an armed escort. The escort was just firing into the trees as they came along. And they went by us so fast, without the signal from David. Then we checked, David had been hit twice in the chest. He was dead, tangled in the tree.*"

"*They didn't even know we were there or that David had been shot. We've never seen anything like that before,*" added William.

"Where's David now?" asked George

"Buried. In woods," Saco responded, still choked up.

Tom pulled John aside and whispered, "See, Amateurs, like I said. That firing into the trees by the escort is a standard procedure of the SS when transporting officials through areas where they may be ambushed."

The rest of the day for Marino, Saco and William was spent mostly silence. They went through several bottles of potato vodka, trying to drown the pain of having lost their teammate.

The next few days passed as the previous ones, except Marino, Saco and William continued to consume a lot of potato vodka. They also did notice a reduction in the street patrols which coincided with the news of the invasion. Tom had been right in that the invasion would cause changes in the priorities of the local troops. It appeared as if some of them had been redeployed.

On June 9th, Peter came in with news. "I have a message for you. Your target has been confirmed as Cuxhaven, and it has to be tomorrow night."

"Thank you," said Tom. "We'll need to leave tomorrow afternoon. Can you arrange for us to stop at the farm again for dinner?"

"Yes," said Peter. "I'll arrange it."

Chapter 31

Tom, George and John spent the evening indulging in potato vodka with Marino, Saco and William. Tom told Marino's trio that after they reached Cuxhaven, they would go their separate ways. Tonight would be their last night together so they made a bit of a party out of it.

In the morning, they all slept late because their heads were aching from the drinks they had. By noon, they were all up and about. The office ladies brought lunch and they all forced themselves to eat a full meal, knowing it could be a long day.

"When we get to Cuxhaven, we will need to steal another boat," Tom said to Marino. "I suggest that I go with William to do that, and then we'll meet you, John, George and Saco at that same secluded beach area."

"First we deliver shell casings," replied Marino. "It is cover for trip. Truck will be full of casings from factory."

"In Cuxhaven?" asked George

"No," replied Marino, "Bremen. Close Cuxhaven. On way."

"Okay, let's load up and get underway."

They began carrying their belongings down to the truck. Saco and Marino started talking in Polish.

"*Something is wrong with them,*" said Saco. "*They are going back to Cuxhaven for their target. Why? What could be there?*"

"*I don't know. Maybe something has moved to there,*" replied Marino.

"*Yes. I know what has moved to there. A submarine. I think they are just leaving,*" said Saco.

Marino thought for a moment. "*Fine. We'll let them leave. William will help them steal the boat, but we will keep their equipment as payment. I have been curious about what is in those boxes.*"

John had been following them through the factory. He was having a hard time keeping a straight face. He didn't want to give them a clue that he knew what they were planning. He was dying to tell George and Tom what he had heard.

The ride to Kolobrzeg was quiet and they were not stopped by a patrol between Gdansk and Kolobrzeg. When they arrived at the farm in Kolobrzeg, Marino, Saco and William went into the farmhouse. John grabbed Tom and George and slowed them down.

"You were right," John said quietly, "they aren't on our team. They are planning to double-cross us."

"What did you hear?" Tom whispered back to John.

"When we meet again after stealing the boat, they are planning to leave us with the boat and take the cargo."

"Okay," said Tom. He quickly worked out a plan in his head. "I think I know how to handle them. Just do as they say and it will all work out."

"Okay, I will," said George, "but now, can you tell us what the hell we are doing?"

"Leaving," replied Tom. "Tonight."

"But we haven't done anything," responded George. "What are we doing with the cargo?"

"It's going with us," replied Tom. "The invasion was successful. They don't need us contaminating parts of Germany now. You, of all people, should have realized that we have enough gas, if used simultaneously, to destroy all of Germany. It can't be left with these amateurs."

"I thought I was the only one that knew that," said George. "In fact, I've calculated that there could be enough to cover well over two hundred thousand square miles."

Suddenly, almost like a light bulb exploding, George realized the true purpose of the mission. "They wanted us to annihilate all of Germany if the invasion failed," George said. "I never dreamed that anyone could go to that extreme. It would be criminal."

"What are you saying?" said John, looking a little confused.

"We didn't know the real range of a pyramid when we left Canada, nor did the war committee when they ordered it. We had estimates but nothing concrete. I've figured out now that we have enough gas right here to wipe out most of Europe. Not just enough to win the war, but to turn most of Europe into a wasteland."

They quickly went inside. They didn't want to be too far behind Marino, Saco and William to avoid arousing any suspicions. Inside, Tom inhaled his food like he had never eaten before. He finished well before the others.

"I'm stuffed," he said. "I'm going outside to get fresh air. Don't be much longer. We need to get going and it looks like we won't get to Cuxhaven before eleven o'clock." Tom went out the front door. Inside everyone heard the sounds of a chair moving across the patio, followed by Tom relaxing in the chair.

The others finished eating and came outside to find Tom snoozing in the chair on the porch. They laughed together as they woke him, then everyone got back into the truck and got underway again.

The drive to Bremen and then Cuxhaven was also uneventful. It was clear that the invasion had impacted the internal patrols because they did not get stopped at all. In Cuxhaven, they followed the plan Tom had laid out. Tom and William went to the docks. They were surprised to find that the very same barge that they had used before was now moored at the docks again.

William laughed, "This easy. We use again."

They silently detached the boat from the docks, started the motor and quickly exited the harbour. It only took a few minutes for them to get the boat into the shallows at the meeting area. They jumped into the knee deep water and pulled the boat far enough onto the sand that it would not drift.

The others were waiting for them on the shore. They had not started to unload the cargo and Tom immediately saw why - Marino and Saco had drawn pistols.

When they were all ashore, Marino kept the pistol trained on their group.

"We go now with truck. Take your boat and go," he told them.

"You can't take the pyramids," George yelled at them "You don't know how to handle them. You'll kill yourselves and everyone around you."

"So, they are deadly," said Saco. "Good. We not stupid. We figure out how to use them. We have many Germans to kill for David."

With that, the three backed up and climbed into the cab. William started the truck, backed the truck away and turned the truck around. As soon as the vehicle had turned, Tom ran, dove and caught hold of the bumper. The truck drove away dragging Tom behind it. George and John stayed standing there, hands in the air, bewildered.

"Now what do we do?" asked John.

"Wait I guess. Just hope Tom comes back soon," George replicd. "Let's wait with the boat."

A few minutes later, Tom came running back through the trees.

"You couldn't stop them?" asked John.

"I wasn't trying to stop them," Tom panted. "I was igniting the present I left for them. I used a magnesium fuse from one of the training pyramids. Ran it into the gas tank. I don't know how long it will take. I had to guess at the length to be a few minutes, but it should explode any..."

Before Tom could finish the sentence, there was a loud explosion from beyond the trees.

"Now," Tom said with a shrug of his shoulders, "do you think that was sufficient to destroy all the pyramids?"

They could see smoke and flames leaping above the tree line.

"Yes," said George, "that should do it. An explosion that large would have easily melted all the plastic and burned off the gas."

"You did all that when you chased the truck?" asked John.

"Heck no," replied Tom. "I set it up while we were at the farm. Right after I ate dinner. I just had to ignite it. When you told us what they were planning, I came up with a plan of my own. It's unfortunate that they forced me to execute it, and well, them."

"That explosion will have attracted attention," said George. "I think we should get away from here before anyone comes. Let's push the boat out and wait offshore for the submarine."

Chapter 32

The trio pushed the barge off the beach and drove it about a mile from the shore. In the dead of night, without any lights, the only bit of the shore they could see was the area where the light from the burning truck shone through the trees. They cut the engines and let the boat drift. After a while, when the light from shore had died down, they began the signal pattern, waiting fifteen minutes between rounds. Eventually, their signal was answered and they started the boat and headed towards the submarine.

When they arrived at the submarine, there was no need for the coded greeting. Captain Steve was already on the deck waiting for them. Steve was extremely happy to see that they came back without any of the original cargo.

"What about the barge?" asked Steve, once they were all on the submarine's deck.

"Just let it drift," replied Tom. "It will wash up on shore somewhere. The owners retrieved it when we borrowed it last week. I'm sure they'll find it again."

Everyone went below and the submarine disappeared below the surface and turned west towards England. Steve explained that they could not follow the Iceland route back as they had been out too long without resupply. They would have to get refuelled in Britain.

The next four weeks were as mundane as they could be on a submarine. They stopped for a day for refuelling at the Rosyth Dockyard on the west coast of Scotland, but everyone stayed close to the submarine. There was no time allotted for touring about the area.

As they got close to Halifax, Tom gathered Steve, George and John into Steve's meeting room. Tom waited until everyone was seated and then began. "I've been through these type of missions before. When we get back to Toronto we will be summoned for a debriefing with the war committee. Steve, I think we need to know what you've reported to Coastal Command and your government."

"Sure," said Steve. "My reports say that we deployed a weapon that you three provided. I've also reported that you have stated that it was a lethal gas, but I haven't seen any direct evidence to corroborate that claim. For all I know, the patrol ships simply called off their attack and I have no idea if your air quality tests were validated. Basically, my report is that I transported you and cargo that may have been a gaseous weapon of undetermined strength."

"You don't believe the gas stopped the attack?" asked John. "The ships just left for other reasons?"

"I'm from Missouri. You'd have to show me." replied Steve. "If the bombs had exploded and sunk the ships like I was expecting, I could confirm that. But I didn't see ships of dead sailors going away from us, I just saw ships."

"Thanks. I guess that won't draw any real questions from your government," said Tom. "Now, can you let us have an all Canadian meeting? We have a few confidential things to discuss about what happened on land."

"Sure," said Steve as he got up and left. "The room is yours for as long as you need it."

When the Canadians were all alone, George asked the question that had been on John and George's minds. "Before we start, can you finally tell us exactly what the plan was? Clearly Gears and I had no idea what we were really doing. We thought the underground was to be given the pyramids and that we'd be training them on their use."

"That's what we all were told," replied Tom, "but I was given this sealed letter and instructed to open it when we reached Germany."

Tom continued as he handed the letter to George. "The Allies had been planning the invasion for quite a while. They knew if it failed, Hitler would have little resistance in conquering England, and then North America. Our actual mission was to make a wasteland of Germany if the invasion failed. Actually, I'm breaking orders by telling you that, but I guess it's alright since you've already figured it out."

John and George exchanged glances that were mixed with horror and relief. After letting the potential gravity of the mission sink in John asked, "So now what?"

"As I said, there will be a debriefing meeting, likely in Ottawa, shortly after we get back. Don't be surprised if they grab the whole team and all the research notes," Tom cautioned.

"And if we don't give them the notes?" asked George.

"I don't know," replied Tom. "I doubt they've ever been told 'no' before. I don't know what they can do, apart from maybe level a treason charge."

"I have no intention of turning over the instrument of Armageddon to a group that contemplated its mass deployment. We're not military or political strategists. When we developed it, we only thought of its use in limited quantities. Clearly, they recognized from our reports that it could be used on a far grander scale."

"But they were only planning to use it if it was absolutely necessary," Tom countered.

"This time," said John with a pause, "but what about next time? I think we need to doctor the notes to mask the chemicals and quantities. They can have everything else."

Chapter 33

When the submarine arrived off the cost of Halifax, a boat was sent from CFB Halifax to meet them. The trio said a heartfelt goodbye to Steve and his crew and jumped into the boat. When they got ashore, Tom went immediately to the motor pool and signed out a jeep. It was already mid-afternoon when they left for Toronto.

Tom sped through the night, stopping only for gas and coffee, letting George and John sleep most of the way. They arrived at the university at about eight-thirty in the morning. At that time, only Ian was there in the offices. Tom left George and John and went to Lily's to get some sleep.

"Good Morning Ian," George said as they came into the office.

"Guys! Welcome Back!" Ian exclaimed.

"Has anything happened while we were gone?" asked John.

"No," replied Ian. "It's been pretty quiet. In fact, I've reassigned almost everyone to other projects."

"Good," said George. "John and I will be in the lab. When Rick comes in, send him to see us please, and have Shelley round up all the notes from our research."

"Why?" asked Ian. "What's going on?"

"Tom expects that we will have our notes seized and sealed by the government. We can't give them the gas formula," George said with such conviction that Ian immediately understood this was the right decision.

"Wait, sit for a moment. I have some news to tell you," Ian said.

When George and John had pulled up the guest chairs and sat, Ian continued. "Rick will not be coming in. He died."

"What!!? When? How?" questioned George.

"He had an abdominal cancer. He had been hiding that he had not been feeling well. He didn't want to let his health slow down our production. Right after you left, he went to see his doctor. It didn't take long for them to diagnose that he had cancer and that it was very advanced. Just before the end of June, he went home early, feeling exhausted. The next morning, he checked into the hospital, and two days later, it was all over. It was like someone just flipped a switch and his whole body shut down," Ian paused, his eyes brimming with tears. "At least it was fairly quick. The family held a private funeral, but we've waited to hold a memorial until you returned. Shelley will set it up for the next weekend."

George and John sat quietly for a moment, absorbing the weight of the news they had just been told. Finally, John spoke. "Well, that's not the homecoming we wanted."

"Yeah," added George, "and he was so young too. Thirty-two? Thirty-Three? He hid it well. I don't remember him working any slower."

"He had just turned thirty-three." Ian paused, drew a deep breath and rallied the group back to the pressing matter at hand. "Okay. I'll have Shelley get the files and meet you in the lab."

When Ian came to the lab and they were waiting for Shelley to have some students bring all the boxes of notes to the lab, George and John told Ian about the order that Tom had

161

been given. Ian realized that they had never contemplated how potentially dangerous FluorZi could be.

"How much area could have been affected?" Ian asked.

"Over the sea, two of them created a cloud that was easily twenty-five miles in radius. That's about two thousand square miles."

"So one hundred of them could cover a hundred thousand square miles," said John, doing the obvious math.

"No, far worse I think," said George. "There's a chance that some of the gas was released and neutralized before the pyramids surfaced. And then, over the ocean, a significant amount would have been reacting with the surface of the water on a continuous basis. That wouldn't happen on land. All things considered, on land, the spread could easily be doubled, perhaps even as much as four or five times. Ian, when we first reported the gas to the war committee, how did you describe its potency?"

"I didn't provide any empirical data, only that a cup full could destroy a small city. I estimated it could make a gas cloud twenty to thirty miles in diameter."

"I guess that's why they ordered a hundred units," said George. "They were guessing that would be sufficient. Your estimate would have seemed reasonable to us at the time, but our experience has now shown that the estimate was way too low."

When the boxes of notes arrived, George and John divided up the boxes and set about redacting all the formula references from the notes. John, being the engineer, was given the boxes associated with the production, just to make sure the final formula was not anywhere in those notes. John wasn't sure about the exact makeup of the formula, but he blackened everywhere he saw a chemical reference. The pair worked quietly and were able to get through all the boxes before leaving for the night. After the work was done, John went directly to see Lily and George raced home in time to put Neville and Betty to bed with a story about three bears and kisses on the foreheads.

Chapter 34

The next morning, when John, George, Tom, Ian, and Robert arrived at the campus, the CFMPs were waiting. As Tom had predicated, the CFMPs were there to escort them and their notes to the debriefing meeting in Ottawa. To Tom's surprise, the attendance of the graduate students had not been required.

They spent the night at a hotel in Ottawa. In the morning they met with a federal government member of the war committee, Steven Stobieman, and General Stephen Rashbee who was a military advisor to the war committee.

They opened the meeting with introductions and handshakes, then they all sat around a large boardroom table.

"Let's begin with the details of the mission to Germany," Stobieman asked.

"It was not too exciting," reported Tom. "We had to deploy two of the gas pyramids to thwart an attack on the submarine during the trip there, but otherwise, we just went ashore and stayed with the underground until we were ordered to return. Unfortunately, our underground contacts tried to keep the remaining pyramids, and in preventing them from doing so, we had to destroy them with a fuel explosion. The trip home on the submarine was also uneventful. And here we are."

"Am I to understand that all of the pyramids are gone?" Stobieman asked.

"Yes," replied George. "The explosion was sufficient to destroy all of them."

"But we could make more if necessary," interjected Rashbee.

"No," said Ian. "We've now realized that the gas is too dangerous to be used and we won't be involved in making any more of it."

"But we could assign it to be made from the research notes," responded Stobieman.

"No, we've removed the formula from the notes. It isn't written down anywhere anymore," said George with a steely look on his face.

"When the hell did you do that?" asked Rashbee.

"Yesterday," responded George.

"That's treasonous," Rashbee said angrily. "We demand you turn over the formula with the notes." He pushed a notepad over towards Robert and John as they were seated the closest to him. "Write it down now."

Robert pushed it back. Waving his thumb back and forth between John and himself, he said, "Sorry, we're engineers. We could tell you how the deployment pyramids work, but that's all we know."

"What about you?" Rashbee said looking at Tom. "You're a soldier. You were involved in the production. I could order you to divulge the formula."

"You could," replied Tom, "but my involvement was mixing this 'stuff' with that other 'stuff'. I couldn't tell you what any of the 'stuffs' were."

"And that leaves just us, the chemists," interjected Ian. "George and Rick invented it, and Rick has passed away. George and I are united in our commitment to keep the formula a secret. In fact, I was only involved in the final production stages. I have a reasonable idea of how it's made, but I don't actually know the exact formula."

"And you?" asked Stobieman.

"I know it, I invented it and I'll likely never forget it." George looked at Stobieman and glared, "But I'll also never repeat it again."

"I would advise you to reconsider. It would be in your best interest," Stobieman said calmly.

"This is your last chance," Rashbee demanded, looking at George. "Write it down now or we will have you charged with treason."

George stared at him for a very long moment. Then he eased and grabbed the notepad and began writing.

"Fine," he said as he wrote. "Here it is."

Rashbee took the pad when George was done and read the formula, "Fluorine, uranium, carbon, potassium, di-uranium. Is that it?"

Ian tried not to laugh, but failed.

"Yes, that's how I remember it," George said with a grin that he couldn't hide.

Stobieman looked from Ian back to George. Pointing at George, he said calmly, "You're trying my patience. In a moment, I am going to call in a guard and have you arrested for treason."

George looked him squarely in the eyes. "Go right ahead," he said, "but you'll never be able to get a conviction without your plans to commit the genocide of all of Germany, and much of Europe, becoming public."

166

Stobieman stiffened. "I don't know what you're talking about."

"Yes, you do. I figured it out," said George, protecting Tom's leak of his orders. "There's no other reason that we would be there with those quantities of the most toxic gas ever created. I saw a map. There aren't enough target cities to have needed a hundred units. A hundred was a good guess that it would be enough to annihilate all Germany. But in fact, based on the results of the two we did deploy in the North Sea, we had enough gas to wipe out most of Europe, not just Germany."

"And I," added Tom, protecting George, "would testify to that. I'm a Canadian Forces Officer and my testimony would be accepted as the truth. After all, those were the exact orders I received."

Stobieman and Rashbee starred at George and Tom for several moments. Tom and George starred back with equal intensity. The room was completely silent. Finally, Stobieman's expression lightened.

"It seems," he said, "we've reached a stalemate. Fine. Here's what we're going to do. We're going to seal the records and your research documents. Your research, mission and this meeting .... Never happened. And you lot, you're going to swear to secrecy on this. And you," he finished, looking at George, "are going to keep your word that you will take the formula to your grave."

They all agreed and Stobieman lead them through an oath of secrecy. As soon as everyone was sworn, Stobieman called the CFMPs to take them back to Toronto.

As they left the meeting, Tom whispered to Ian, "What was that formula George wrote?"

"That formula..." Ian laughed. He then whispered to Tom, "What you need to remember is that the symbol for Potassium is 'K', and 'Di' means two, so if you write the formula using the chemical symbols, it is F-U-C-K-U$_2$," and Ian again started laughing lightly.

Tom started to laugh too. Through the laughter he managed to get out, "Well, when they figure that out, they might want to reconsider our deal."

Chapter 35

The rain had let up and Neville could see down the road again. He pulled out from under the bridge and back onto the highway, heading for George's house.

George continued the story.

"After that, the CFMPs took us back to Toronto. We never heard from Stobieman, Rashbee or any of the war committee again."

"The following weekend, we had the memorial for Rick and then Gears and Lily were married about two weeks after that. Both Lily and your mother passed within the last couple of years, as you know, but Bounce and Gears and I have stayed close ever since we got back from that trip."

"Wait," interrupted Neville, "did you ever find out where the name Bounce came from?"

"Oh yeah," laughed George. "It was not as exciting as you might think. It turns out that on his very first parachute training jump, Tom got stuck upside down in a tree. He pretty much landed on his noggin when he got himself out of the harness. His platoon gave him that nickname as a reminder of the event."

Neville took a moment to absorb everything that he had just been told. "Well, that's a hell of a story. At least now I know where your nicknames came from."

For the rest of the drive back to George's home, George regaled Neville with his memories of the other people involved in his adventure. Some, like Captain Hannan, he had never encountered again. Others, like his university teammates, George had kept in touch with and had followed their careers. The biggest surprise was that Dr. Daniel Davids had gone on to develop a line of pet foods and had become quite wealthy. And he married his date from the New Year's Eve party after she got her doctorate in psychology.

For the next two decades, George continued to visit Neville, Mary and Henry. But, as all good things must come to an end, the end came for Tom, John and eventually George over those twenty years.

George had been a huge influence on Henry, and Henry followed in his grandfather's footsteps, earning his BSc in chemistry from the University of Toronto, shortly before George passed. Henry was an exceptional chemist and he quickly earned his MSc in chemistry as well. After that, he moved on to working on his PhD, also at the University of Toronto.

One New Year's Eve, Henry attended the party put on by the university for faculty and graduate students. At this party, Henry met a beautiful Asian student named Lan Wan who had come from Changsha to work on her MSc in architecture. Henry was in love from the moment he saw her. It took some effort on his part before Lan finally agreed to date him. But within a year, they were married.

In the year following Lan's completion of her MSc, Henry and Lan were the proud parents of a beautiful daughter that they named Eileen. Neville and Mary were the typical doting grandparents and were often at Henry's home. By the time Eileen was three, she had developed a special relationship with Neville.

One day, Neville was sitting in Henry's family room in a recliner with Eileen seated on his lap. Henry came into the room. "I keep hearing lots of laughter. What are you two doing?" he asked.

Neville smiled. "Just talking. She's smart, like Einstein."

A flash of a memory hit Neville and he started to laugh.

"What?" asked Henry, looking around himself, thinking Neville was laughing at him.

"I was just remembering, I had almost the exact same conversation with my father about you when you were about four or five," Neville said. "Did you know, I met Einstein once, but I don't remember it. I was too young. He was a friend of my father's."

"Interesting," responded Henry. "I guess they were both professors around the same time."

"This conversation also reminds me of a story that I should have told you a while ago. Pull up a chair, this story is a little long."

Henry slid the chair from the family room furniture set closer to the recliner.

"This is the story about your grandfather's activity during WWII. It was classified as top secret and he made me swear that I wouldn't tell this story until after he died. I guess I could have told you a few years ago, but it's a long story to tell. I hope you don't have anywhere to be for a little while."

Henry told Neville that he didn't and Neville began to recount George's adventures during the war. When he was finished, he said, "I swore that I wouldn't do anything with the story until after he was gone. Well, now I've passed it to you. What will you do with it?"

Henry responded, "It's a hell of a story, Dad. Perhaps I'll turn it into a book."

Addendum

My father, Dr. James T. Burt-Gerrans, Prof. Emeritus of the University of Toronto, was a physical chemist who was the director of a secret research project which involved the halogen Fluorine. At that time, it was believed to be involved in the splitting of the atom. Whether that research or the halogen ever was involved in the actual production of the atomic bomb, I have no idea.

However the work done by 5 graduate students, working under my father's direction, produced, probably by accidental experimentation, a weapon of mass destruction. This weapon was a gas, liquid below 70F degrees and so powerful in the gaseous state above 70F degrees, a seemingly small volume could produce a sterile, lifeless planet Earth!

The only people in the world who knew of this substance or it's power were my father, the 5 graduate students, the executive of the National Research Council of Canada, Prime Minister King, MP C. D. Howe and, by secured communications, Winston Churchill. My father also contacted Albert Einstein, whom he had met several times at scientific meetings, explained the total history and results of experimentation with the gas at a secret and private meeting. According to my father, two of the graduate students were killed by the gas in the laboratory.

In meetings with the Canadian officials, my father refused to divulge the formula or the production process. Under the threat of treason, he secretly arranged to have all the research materials burned. Both Einstein and Churchill agreed that the substance was too dangerous to be used in military operations. The only existing sample of the gas was sealed in a concrete block and under the supervision of my father, and with the assistance of a British submarine, the sample was disposed of in the Atlantic Ocean.

Shortly before his death, my father told me the whole story as, at that time, all the people in the "need to know" were dead and there was absolutely no record of the method of production of the gas. All the paperwork, even scraps of information on the back of an envelope or scratch pad, had been burned on the orders of my father.

To illustrate how seriously this substance was taken by those who knew of it, one member of the National Research Council said to my father, "Sir, You hold ARMAGEDDON in your hands."

Dr. Norman E. Burt-Gerrans

CPSIA information can be obtained
at www.ICGtesting.com
Printed in the USA
LVOW07s2029041017
551145LV00002B/2/P